D0506760

The Last Matriarch

SHARMAN APT RUSSELL

The Last Matriarch A Novel

University of New Mexico Press ✷ Albuquerque

Library of Congress Cataloging-in-Publication Data
Russell, Sharman Apt.
The Last Matriarch/Sharman Apt Russell—1st edition

  p. cm.
  ISBN 0–8263–2131–3 (cloth)

  1. Paleo-Indians—North America Fiction.
  2. Mammoths—North America Fiction.
  3. Clovis culture Fiction.
   I. Title.
PS3568.U776 L37 2000
813'.54—dc21   99-6657
CIP

Designed by Sue Niewiarowski
Illustrations by Aaron Campbell

To David Grant Russell

Introduction

This story takes place in southern New Mexico, where I live today. As much as possible I have tried to create the physical world of the American Southwest approximately 11,000 years ago. At that time, herds of camels, llamas, horses, bison, four-horned antelope, and mammoths grazed the plains of sweet, long-season grass. Their predators included lions, cheetahs, giant short-faced bears, dire wolves, and saber-toothed cats. It was a world measured on a different scale. Ground sloths lumbered about like rhinoceros. Beavers weighed three hundred pounds.

The Clovis people also lived here. We know these men and women hunted mammoths, mastodon, and giant bison because we have found spear points in ancient rib cages. Researchers agree that these people used the same brain we use. They are us.

In South America, at an archaeological site dated to 12,800 B.P. (before present), people built rectangular huts with log foundations and pole frameworks draped in animal skins. The recovered items include wooden mortars, worked bone, ivory tools, a cache of salt, mastodon remains, and chewed medicinal leaves.

So, too, my Clovis characters have many different skills. They count easily up to ten. Their language is complex. Some of them, if they escape injury or disease, enjoy a relatively long life.

2   In part this book was inspired by an archaeological debate: Did human hunters or climate change cause the extinction of nearly eighty percent of our large land mammals at the end of the Pleistocene? Today thousands of species are also disappearing. Biologists predict that animals like the wild elephant will be gone in the next century. It is hard to imagine such a loss.

I think it was *as* hard at 11,000 B.P. in the American Southwest.

Geneology

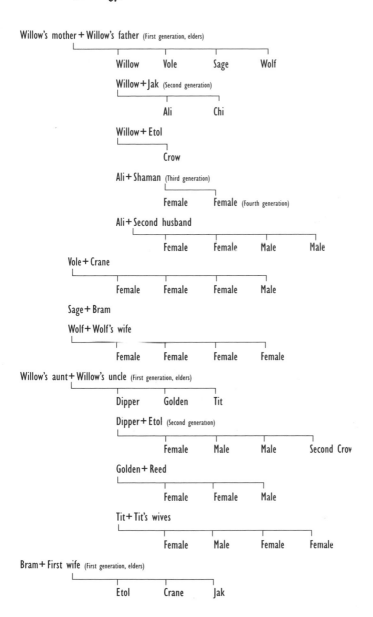

Willow's mother + Willow's father (First generation, elders)

Willow   Vole   Sage   Wolf

Willow + Jak (Second generation)

Ali   Chi

Willow + Etol

Crow

Ali + Shaman (Third generation)

Female   Female (Fourth generation)

Ali + Second husband

Female   Female   Male   Male

Vole + Crane

Female   Female   Female   Male

Sage + Bram

Wolf + Wolf's wife

Female   Female   Female   Female

Willow's aunt + Willow's uncle (First generation, elders)

Dipper   Golden   Tit

Dipper + Etol (Second generation)

Female   Male   Male   Second Crov

Golden + Reed

Female   Female   Male

Tit + Tit's wives

Female   Male   Female   Female

Bram + First wife (First generation, elders)

Etol   Crane   Jak

Extinct Late Pleistocene North American Mammals

American cheetah
American lion
American mastodon
Aztlan rabbit
Dhole*
Diminutive pronghorn
Elk-moose
Flat-headed peccary
Florida cave bear*
Giant beaver
Giant short-faced bear
Harlan's ground sloth
Harlan's musk ox
Holmes's capybara*
Horses*
Jefferson's ground sloth
Large-headed llama
Long-nosed peccary
Mammoths
Mountain deer
Northern pampathere

Pinckney's capybara
Rusconi's ground sloth
Saber-toothed cat
Saiga*
Scimitar cat
Shasta ground sloth
Short-faced skunk
Shrub ox
Shuler's pronghorn
Simpson's glyptodont
Southern pampathere
Stout-legged llama
Tapirs*
Yesterday's camel

5

Genus survives outside North America

Part One

Chapter One

My husband has a bad relationship with plants but a good one with animals. His skin animal was the lion. When we discovered this, we knew he would hunt mammoths. Only lions kill the baby mammoths. Only humans prey on the adults. My husband helped spear four mammoths in as many years before he died, his chest crushed by the matriarch of the herd.

Etol told me the story, sitting by Jak's grave and letting that place know what kind of bones rested there. Four of them had gone hunting—Jak; his father, Bram; his brother, Etol; and my cousin Golden. They followed the herd for three days, hoping that one of the mammoths would wander off alone. Sometimes a female tries to find a mate. Sometimes a bull decides to leave his family group. This is what happened. When the animal was far enough away, Bram teased him into charging while Jak, Golden, and Etol threw their spears. Jak's thrust entered the rib cage behind the shoulder and went into the lungs. Golden hit leg muscle and splintered bone. Etol's spear passed through the ribs into the stomach. As the male fell, his organs collapsed under his weight. In a moment, the bull was dead.

Bram quickly cut the hide, letting heat and gases escape. Golden felt for the fat around the young bull's kidney. This was a healthy, well-fed animal! The three hunters found their weapons. Golden's foreshaft had snapped, and Jak's point needed to be reshaped. All the while, they watched for predators and for the herd who might come to mourn the bull's death. Mammoths can speak to each other over long distances. For this reason, the killing site should have plenty of cover as well as firewood if the meat has to be guarded.

When the matriarch came walking through scrub brush and sweet grass, she was a huge beast, taller than a family's summer tent. Her tusks curved out and down and up, each one as long as a man. Jak and the others hid in the bushes, knowing this would be a weary time of waiting as the mammoths prodded their companion, tried to lift him, smelled his body, trumpeted, and wept. Their grief is strong as long as it lasts. Eventually they would swing their feet, a sign of indecision. Then the matriarch would rumble and the herd move away heavily, slowly, touching each other for comfort. They would make no effort to find the hunters or drive them off. Mammoths are not interested in revenge.

Only this time, the matriarch must have felt differently. Perhaps it was a favorite son lying on the ground with his stomach open, his body already cut and eaten. Also, as I say, my husband has a bad relationship with plants. Perhaps the grasses parted to show his trail or the scrub brush refused to hide his face. Certainly the matriarch saw him—and still she did not attack. Later Etol worried about that the most.

If the mammoth had charged then, Jak would have stood with his spear and Etol with his atlatl. With luck they might have brought her down, escaping in the herd's confusion. Instead the matriarch cried, shuffled, and moved slyly closer to Jak's hiding place. The sun rose two fingers in Old Man's sky. Mammoths cannot see behind them without turning, and the matriarch kept her back to Jak so that he chose to stay hidden, like the fawns of black-striped antelope. When she suddenly swung and came at a rush, he was surprised. She killed him in a gallop, her feet on his ribs, his heart pushed into the earth.

Bram and Etol carried back the body, which we covered with red ochre and buried with Jak's spear and atlatl, his bone shaft wrench, his ivory, and fluted points. As my son watched, I added two cores of good-quality chert from a quarry five days away. I could have struck flakes and points from those cores all winter. My son, a few summers past weaning, wanted me to give a tusk from the dead mammoth, since one of these was now mine. But I kept this prize, thinking I would need it to trade for more chert and the lost bone shaft wrench.

My daughter, who was older, understood. She went to the smallest hill near our camp to gather yucca leaves. Cleverly she wove a loose basket to sit by her father's shoulder. Into that we put sage, pine needles, and willow bark.

My son could have chosen to make his own gift. Etol and I explained this to the oak tree by my husband's grave. We explained it to the bones themselves, who listened patiently, more patient than the man they had once carried. My son did not behave well at the burial. Crying, he ran from his uncles and his grandfathers. His tantrum was his only gift.

We look at our life as though it were a journey and we try to see those trails again, remembering where we chose to turn here or there. I have often thought about the anger my son has toward me now. Sometimes I think it started when I would not give the mammoth tusk to my husband's body. I kept that to trade for a bone shaft wrench.

But this is too simple an explanation. Why, after all, *was* I so stingy?

My skin plant is willow. Not all of us know what plant or animal or stone we carry under our skin, and most of my relatives wait for their death to find out. Still, I am willow, my husband was lion, and no one thought we would be a good match. We coupled when I was barely past menses. My daughter was born two years later, a strong, healthy girl from a man who was also strong, healthy, and well respected. I stayed with my husband because I wanted these things for my children. Also, there were not many men to choose from, only two younger boys from the people across the big river. My son does not understand the problems we buy with a marriage gift, or maybe he understands them too well. At that time, he saw it clearly. I was at fault because I did not love his father enough.

Soon after Jak's death, I began hunting for meat and skins. I could have gotten these things from my brothers and fa-

ther, but that would have meant obligations, trading, perhaps another marriage. I preferred to live alone in my summer tent. Willow likes me, and my aim is good. Because of
the children, I did not hunt dangerous game. Instead I went
after deer, antelope, tapirs, peccaries, rabbits, armadillos, and
the slow-moving tortoise. I traveled always with a partner
or in a group, often with Etol and my cousin Golden. For
practice I killed the bad-tasting ground sloth. I worked hard
to find the right length and weight for my willow spear, holding that little tree through the night, talking to it in the morning when the animals also begin to think about food.

All this was good because my children and I continued to
have the status of hunters, with meat to cook and skins to
sew. Today I see this was possible because of my sister, Sage,
with whom I traded to watch my son and daughter while I
was gone. I also gave hides to her husband, Bram, my father-
in-law, to help carry our supplies when we moved camp.
Sometimes my son, Chi, would pretend to feel neglected, especially when he wanted a treat or extra food. In truth, he
loved his aunt, who had no children of her own. My daughter took on the task of gathering our plants, the lamb's-
quarter, acorns, plums, and yucca root. Most girls do this,
but Ali was especially industrious. She gave me even more
freedom to hunt.

During these years, I often saw the mammoth herd, not
as a hunter but as someone who shares the plain. The first
time, one late afternoon, Etol and I lay on a rise overlook-
ing a green marsh. Mixed among a herd of small horses were

four-horned antelope flashing patterns of yellow and black. Camels grazed on the herd's edge, not liking the horses, but using them to watch for saber-toothed cats, cheetahs, lions, and us. Briefly in the blue sky the wings of condors blocked the sun. When the big birds found a dying animal or a dead one, they would be joined by red-necked vultures and teratorns. Rich in grass, rich in meat, we are a chosen people in a chosen land. It was not always like this.

Trying to ignore the ants and flies, Etol and I wormed forward on our stomachs, planning the hunt. Sweet-smelling grass rustled above our heads. A little behind us, Golden kept watch.

"You are lucky," Etol suddenly whispered, and then I heard them too, a large group of mammoths trumpeting down a nearby hill. They ran sloppily, trunks flopping, little tails swishing, heads held high. When they reached the marsh, the calves wriggled in the mud until their brown, red, and gray coats turned glistening black. The older females also came running but behaved more delicately near the water. In silence, they went to the clear stream that entered the marsh, dipped the tips of their trunks, and squirted liquid down their throats.

The group was happy to find such a nice mud hole. One calf fell to her knees, and another climbed on her back and head. This became their favorite game, climbing and tumbling until they made a messy heap. The younger females acted frisky while the bulls began to spar, pushing each other, their tusks knocking. The horses, camels, and antelope had already rushed away. Now, at some distance, they turned to stare. In a moment they were grazing again, safer than before, so close to the mammoth herd.

Etol touched my shoulder. Walking at the rear of her family group, the matriarch moved slowly down the grassy hill, past clumps of pine and juniper trees that she made seem smaller. Discreetly the others stood aside when she came to the stream and dipped her trunk. These mature females were her daughters and granddaughters. Five or six adolescent males, her sons and grandsons, also lived with the herd. Then there was the heap of wiggling babies, each one descended from her line.

"We call her Half Ear," Etol whispered.

Mammoth ears are not large, but watching carefully, I could see that the old one's ear had been partly cut, perhaps by a spear. She was the largest female on the plain, higher than one man standing on the shoulder of another, thicker than five men linked together.

We waited while the herd fed, twisting their trunks around the water grass, ripping it free, stuffing it in their mouths, and reaching for more. After a long time, the matriarch rumbled and walked away from the marsh to higher, dry ground. From a patch of soil, she scooped up the dust with her trunk and blew it over her back. The others followed and did the same. Standing close, they gathered together with hindquarters touching. A reddish brown mammoth lightly rubbed against the matriarch's shoulder. The calves suckled their mothers, until one by one the babies lay down. A few big females looped their trunks like vines around the ivory tusks. Others let their long noses hang down. Hardly a tail moved to scare off the flies.

Etol wanted to leave.

"It's good to watch them," he said, "to see who is here. We don't find mammoths so often. But they are asleep, and I am bored. This place is ruined for hunting."

"How long will they stay?" I asked.

Etol shrugged. "Six fingers."

I wanted to know more. "Have the hunters named them?" Etol nodded. The matriarch had four daughters, Big Ivory, Little Ivory, Red Fur, and Gray Fur. Her other children were grown bulls, enormous creatures larger than the matriarch, who grazed separately in a bachelor herd. In this group, Big Ivory had an unnamed full-grown daughter, an adolescent male named Little Penis, and an unnamed calf. Little Ivory had an adolescent male named Big Penis, a young unnamed female, and an unnamed new calf. Sometimes other females also joined the group.

I wanted to show Etol that I had been listening closely. "Which are the children of Red Fur and Gray Fur?"

Etol squinted at the sleeping mammoths.

"Just like a hunter," I teased. "Look at these names. You are only interested in ivory and penises."

My brother-in-law laughed. We often shared an easy joke. At the same time he shifted slightly so that I could smell the crushed flowers under his thigh. Etol had already asked if I would become his second wife. My father wanted it too and hoped I would agree. But Etol's first wife, Dipper, was a hard woman to live with. For this and other reasons, I asked my father to say no.

The story of the mammoths made me think of my own family. I also come from a strong lineage, the product of two sisters, my mother and aunt, who married two brothers, my father and uncle. My mother gave birth to my sister, Sage, my brother Vole, and me. She died when my brother Wolf was born. My aunt and uncle had two boys, Golden and Tit, and a girl, Dipper. That made us two hands joined together, all related by blood.

One day at a gathering by the big river, another group asked to join us. Bram was the father of Jak, Etol, and Crane. Their mother, like mine, had died in childbirth, and they were unhappy living with her relatives. They also needed husbands and wives, as did some of us. No one spoke of this at the time. Instead we welcomed them for a season of hunting. That summer I coupled with Jak, Etol courted my cousin Dipper, and Crane looked at my brother Vole.

The biggest surprise was Bram and Sage. My sister's first marriage had not produced children, and this husband divorced her when he left our group. Although Bram was as old as my father—and a poor hunter—he carried chert and flint under his skin. Most important, he had children already and did not seem to want more.

So, rather quickly, this family joined ours. It turned out as well as anyone could expect. Now we were strong with many adults. In addition, I had Chi and Ali. Vole and Crane had two children, Etol and Dipper had three, and Crane was pregnant again. Our biggest problem was finding wives for my brother Wolf and two cousins Golden and Tit. They wanted to marry, but they did not want to leave our family group.

18   That day I was not a good companion for Etol. We say that thinking is bad for hunting, which is why storytellers and old people get their meat by trade or obligation. To kill game, a hunter's awareness must become a thin net. In this way he will catch all the life around him. We believe that the world is curious about human beings. This land, in particular, loves to listen to our thoughts and catch us suddenly in its net. When we die, we enter the land, and so we are generous about sharing our stories. But when we hunt, those voices inside us can scare the animal we want to eat. When we hunt, we do not tell stories. Our thoughts live in the willow spear or, for a man like my husband, in the animal's flesh.

Etol, my cousin Golden, and I left the mammoths bathing in the mud hole, scrubbing their skin free of pests. We went to a valley close to our summer camp, where Etol speared an antelope and I wounded a long-nosed peccary, which got away. This was not much meat for our families. If my uncle or brothers had done better, Etol knew they would share with him first, for he was an in-law and in-laws must be kept happy, joined to the group. Golden could still eat with his father. My children would fare less well since I had to share with Sage and Bram. Because of this, Etol let me carry the antelope and take most of the meat home.

After that, I watched mammoths whenever I could. One day, I saw this herd meet with another. First, Half Ear's group burst through a wood of large-needled trees, screaming and trumpeting, heads lifted, ears flapping. Now the second family also rushed forward from their place near a small muddy pond. The younger animals clicked tusks, spun, farted, and urinated. Half Ear went straight to the other matriarch, a smaller female with two beautifully curved ivories. Both mammoths held each other's trunks and rumbled.

Hidden in the scrub brush, I watched Red Fur, the favorite daughter of the matriarch, who was nursing a new calf as she tried to wean her second youngest. That husky male had two tiny tusks just beginning to emerge. Following his mother, he hooked his trunk around her leg as a signal that he wanted milk. In the past, Red Fur would have stopped and stretched a leg forward so that her son could easily reach the teat. Now she moved on, gently shaking off the male, who squealed in protest.

Soon both herds began feeding. All this reminded me of my people when we meet at a gathering by the big river. At first our excitement is extreme. We scream and cry and greet friends and relatives, arranging a dance that will go on all night. At my first big dance, clapping with the men and women in a circle, I thought I would die from such strong emotion. So many strangers! So many possibilities! Everyone seemed to feel the same way.

Yet in a few days, the gathering by the river is just another gathering and we behave as we always do. The adults are here to do business. We take care of the children, worry about marriage gifts, and make our trades. We are happy enough to leave when it is time.

20 In the grassy clearing before me, Tiny Tusks squealed until Red Fur gave up and let him nurse. The new calf, twice my weight, suckled on one side. Her smug brother suckled on the other. In the end, Tiny Tusks would be weaned. Still, I recognized in Red Fur a certain weariness. This son would take all her patience.

In the evening, as fresh meat cooked over the coals, I told these stories about Red Fur and Half Ear to my son and daughter. I did not always talk about the mammoth herd. I also showed them lion scat and pellets from the horned owl. I described the play of dire wolves and measured out the length of the giant insect-eater. But it was the mammoths who interested me the most, and this angered Chi.

"Half Ear," he said one night, "killed my father."

Our small fire lit the walls of the tent, made of horse and camel hide. Smoke escaped out the top hole, where three poles met and where I could see the stars. Around me, our furs and tools were stored neatly in their places. I loved these times alone with my children in this flickering light. Our food was peccary and prickly pear fruit. The meat was greasy. The fruit was sweet.

"Yes," I said to Chi. "Half Ear is the matriarch. She killed your father, I think, because he killed her son. Do you want to hear that story again?"

"Yes." Chi stared at me, his jaw jutted, his lip pushed out

in a familiar expression. "No, not really!" Now he shook his head so that the short black hair lifted and fell. "I know the story. The mammoth killed our father, yet you," he accused me, "seem to like her."

Now my daughter, Ali, interrupted. Close to her menses, she had many opinions. "Mother doesn't *like* or *dislike* the matriarch. Half Ear is a mammoth. We don't like or dislike mammoths."

This wise girl was not often wrong. But in truth, I did like Half Ear even though I could not say this out loud, just as my son could not say out loud that he hated her. Something in my chest hurt, yet I knew there was no injury there. My son would never be a good hunter if he carried these feelings onto the plain.

"Ali is right. Hunters do not think like that," I said sharply. This only shamed Chi, and his lip pushed out further. I did not reach over, but I wanted to comfort him.

I see now that this was a fault. I could never take my son's anger seriously. I loved that mouth turned down or up. I loved those eyes shaped like a black cactus seed, the smooth brown skin and perfect flat nose, the small ears and high cheekbones. From his birth, this boy overwhelmed me with his beauty.

Ali gave a loud sigh. "Do you want more meat?" She picked from the ashes the last strip of peccary.

"No!" Chi grunted in triumph as though denying himself meat would make us suffer.

"You eat it," I told my daughter. "Then we will cover the fire and sleep."

Over the coals, I sprinkled sage and a dried yellow flower. The strong good smell made us shiver. My children lay beside me under a bearskin that kept us too warm in the warm season. Jak had killed that bear when we were newly married, and the animal had many stories to tell. She whispered of white grubs and the insides of certain trees. She dreamed of fish so that I might wake in the morning wanting a meal impossible to get at that camp or in that time. More rarely, the bearskin remembered her death, and then I caught the sour odor of Jak's sweat. I saw his dark arms and heard his voice calming the bear, helping her die. I know that Chi loved this skin too, perhaps for these same memories. So we slept under it summer and winter.

These are the moments I carry in bone. Ali lay on one side of me, a woman nearly grown, her hand resting in mine. Chi lay on the other side, as far away as he could get, because he was still angry and wanted me to know that. Sometime in the night he would creep closer to put his head on my breast, just as he did every night when he was a child still nursing. Chi had not nursed now for many years. But when he felt strong emotion, when we had fought and he wanted to make up, he would come close and push his face against me. You are mine, his skin would say, I belong to you.

We slept, the three of us, lightly touching each other for comfort. The eye of Old Woman rose in the sky.

Uuuuuaaaawaugh. A lion hunted in the east.

Chapter Two

That spring, flowers covered the earth like snow. Above our camp, the long flanks of hills turned white. In the other direction, west and south, we looked down from our tents on a pink bluff to a riverbed green with willow, alder, and narrow-leafed trees. Our thoughts moved over the wooded valley floor to the next fold of hills, glimpsed through patches of juniper and little pine. To the north, spruce began where the valley rose into real snow. Directly south, the fang of a sharp-toothed mountain pierced Old Man's sky.

South, too, the long-season grass spread out in the shape of a buffalo robe, furry with growth, swirling in the colors of bull thistle, poppy, and aster. When my children came back from gathering seeds, daisies wreathed their black hair. As serious as if they were working stone, they made necklaces of yucca thread strung with orange, purple, red, lavender, and blue. At night the fragrance filled our tent.

"Mother! Put this on!" Ali held up a circle of yellow.

"Have you been gathering food or flowers?" I waved her away. I wanted to think.

That spring, my father killed a mare and did not see the stallion rush from a gray rock at the canyon's mouth. Fortunately Father turned in time to run a spear through the animal's chest. Even so, one hoof caught him on the shoulder. My aunt nursed him in her tent, grinding herbs and sending Ali to get willow bark for his pain.

In early summer, I approached my uncle. First I waited for Etol and Golden to sit beside him at the central fire under the face of Old Woman. The night was clear and moonless, and the stars told many stories all at once. The beginning of the world glittered above us. Our journey to this land rose in the north.

I had a purpose here, and as I talked I tended a stew at the edge of the embers, salting the meat from my own supply.

"Uncle," I said, handing him a wooden bowl, "I would like to go with you on the next mammoth hunt."

Now the other hunters had their chance to speak. Etol and Golden were silent, which was good. Wolf glanced at me. I had already warned him, my younger brother. I had waited until my older brother, Vole, was in his tent. That left my cousin Tit, who was also silent, only because he was slow with words.

Finally Tit challenged me. "Why would you want that?"

I tried not to sound impatient. "I need marriage gifts. Ali will need a husband soon. I have a son as well."

"Ivory in fall to carve in winter," Etol quoted the old hunter's saying.

Tit frowned. Even he understood that my father would not be able to help me now. Most likely, my father would never hunt mammoths again. Vole had to prepare for his own children and Wolf for his own marriage.

"Ivory is not the only gift," my uncle murmured.

I was careful to keep my voice low. "I want the best."

The cooking fire had died, and I could see my uncle's face dimly in the starlight. He was dressed in undecorated leather pants and shirt, his long braid also plain and undecorated, hanging down his back. The dark creases in his cheeks seemed to deepen. Perhaps he wrinkled his nose. Men do not like to share the mammoth hunt.

Respectfully I kept my eyes down. My uncle and I were not close, but he had lived a long life, and he knew me well. I could plead further or be quiet and let him think. My father had advised me to choose the second.

Secretly, when the women went out to gather plants, they complained about the mammoth hunters. Yes, the meat was tender and tasty. But in this land we had plenty of other meat. In a good season, the herds of grazing animals shook the ground. In a bad season, we killed small creatures in our traps and snares. We killed voles, squirrels, and mice. We ate fruits, nuts, seeds, and roots. When the men hunted mammoths, they were gone for days, leaving their chores for others to do. They risked injury and death and on their return sat talking for hours around the central fire.

Of course men hunted mammoth for ivory, and women also valued the white tusks. We made them into beads, which we strung as necklaces and sewed onto clothing. We made ivory needles, ivory awls, ivory combs, ivory buttons. Sometimes we carved animals and figures, marriage gifts to show off our talent and wealth. We made gifts because we were proud—and the men hunted for the same reason. Only lions and humans dared to kill the shaggy mammoth. In their dances at night, the men sang, "Lions, mammoths, and men. We are the muscles in the body of the land."

I would sing that song too if my uncle agreed. I would have my own tusk to carve this winter so that my daughter could go to the people at the big river and offer them a strong camp. Although she had no father, she would not be ashamed. Although he had no father, my son would not be tempted too early on the plain. Unready, untried, Chi was eager to hunt in Jak's place. I would stand in that place a little longer.

Around the fire, the younger men shifted, curious to hear my uncle's decision.

"What does my brother say?" My uncle spoke at last.

I held back my triumph.

"Go ask my younger brother," my uncle continued. "If he says yes, what can I do? I would never oppose him."

The old man lied shamelessly.

As the wind blew from the north, I spread my net thin to catch it, my shoulder blades stretching out like wings. I smelled with my ears and listened from the corners of my eyes. We had been two days tracking a female, her baby, and an adolescent male. Such a small group was unusual. My uncle believed these mammoths were strangers separated from a distant herd, for they wandered aimlessly past good grazing meadows. I was anxious to prove myself, and the other hunters took advantage of that. At the end of each day, I gathered all the firewood and kept the longest watch. I packed extra supplies and endured the jokes of Wolf and Golden, who saw the sexual parts of men in every hill and rock cropping. In my right hand I carried a new spear, heavier than the old, balanced all summer to my weight.

We followed our prey to a water hole in the curve of a pink canyon. Mammoths need a lot of water, and these animals drank thirstily. As we looked down at them from a ridge, the pink cliffs at the water hole hardly seemed higher than the female's great hairy back. My uncle motioned the way we should descend in the shelter of an arroyo, through the scrub oak and juniper trees. He told Etol, Golden, and Wolf to attack the mother. He and I would strike for the male.

"Your bull will panic," Etol explained to me. "The female may charge, but the others are too young. This is a good hunt. A lot of meat and not much danger." Etol quoted another hunter's saying. He was fond of them.

As thick as my body, the female's tusks curved down and up in a dizzy swoop. With these she could crack a lion's skull or batter a pine tree to the ground. With a toss of her head, she could cut me in half.

"Remember," Etol suddenly warned. "Mammoths can run, as fast as a horse."

Then we were moving from the ridge, creeping over the rocks and sand, smelling leaves and wet earth. As planned, Etol, Wolf, and Golden burst from the thorny bushes and raced toward the drinking mammoths, their spears held high, parallel to the ground. Wolf threw first and hard and swerved back to whatever cover he could find. Etol and Golden took time to aim for the chest and head. One spear hit the animal's shoulder and drove into muscle. Another went through her ear and neck. The third bit into her heart. She screamed. The noise echoed against the rocks.

Some of this I learned later. At the time, I was also jumping from the bushes, finding the young male, and throwing my spear—careful to avoid hitting my uncle! His weapon struck the male's leg and quivered there. My thrust went between two ribs.

The male panicked just as Etol predicted. Squealing, he stumbled to his dying mother, then away from her in horror, back and away before he turned and fled deeper into the canyon. The female screamed again and fell, her legs in the water hole. Nearby her child had been playing happily in the mud. Frantic now, the baby ran to her mother's side and pushed against a hairy thigh. Pathetically she tried to nurse.

The men came out of the brush. Bright red gushed from the female's mouth, and she lay still. I stood where I had rooted. If the male had charged, I would be dead now. Etol wrenched his weapon from the mammoth's neck and used it to quickly kill the child. The air smelled of hot blood and fresh dung. A blue sky glowed behind the pink walls. I quivered like the spear in the male's flesh.

Some part of me grieved for these mammoths. Their cries would enter the crumbling cliffs, and this is one of the stories the canyon would tell, how the humans came to kill the mother and her children.

Mostly, however, I shook from excitement. I had never faced death so closely or deliberately. Relief turned to delight shivering up and down the skin of my arms. Growing stronger, a fierce greed hollowed my stomach. This meat was mine, tender and tasty. I would eat this mammoth fresh, not half spoiled, the leftovers dragged back by other hunters. I would eat from the liver and fatty hump, cooked right here. We would cut open the feet and I would eat the fat that cushions the mammoth when she walks. The ivory was also partly mine! I would have beads to carve, a necklace for my daughter.

I barely heard my uncle talk to the mammoths, explaining to them their deaths. As Wolf and I cut into the hairy coat, through joints and muscle, Etol made a fire. We would take home the tusks and as much meat as we could bring on our backs and two litters. The trunks were especially easy to carry, good sources of fat. Some of the meat we would eat tonight Some we would cache in a pine tree. If the weather stayed cold, Tit and Vole could return for it later.

Unfortunately these mammoths had not been feeding well.

"She's not old," Etol remarked of the mother, "but she's thin."

"And the male?" I asked. "Will we track him?"

"He's traveling too fast. Later he will die from infection. Your spear hit deep."

Etol knew that I lusted for the male's two tusks. As one of the hunting party, I would get a share from this female. But with my spear in his ribs, I would get more from the male. Also I wanted my spear back.

"You will do better next time," Etol promised me.

That night lions came to steal our meat. These lions were not from the pride who shared our hunting grounds. They were two young brothers cast out from their family group, searching to take over a new pride. Our fires kept them back although I could see the tawny shapes uncomfortably close, moving in the shadows under the trees.

They roared at us, *Uuuuuuoooooowaugh! Uuuuooo! Uaooo, uaoooo, oooogh, oooogh, oooogh!*

We roared back! Our meat! Our meat!

They showed us their teeth, and we shook our spears.

If there had been more than two lions, we would have left. Lions often steal from people, although I had never heard of people stealing from lions. Tonight we had too many fires and too many spears, and the males went away angrily, swishing their long tails.

Carrying the meat back was harder than I expected. But when we arrived at the summer camp, my son's face made me feel less tired. Yes, I thought, this is the right thing to do. In this way I am keeping him safe.

My children were happy with mammoth in their stomachs and ivory in our tent. Over and over Chi asked about the hunt, his voice loud and impatient. My fears rose again. There was a rock in this boy I kept pushing against. He had run crying from his father's burial, and I did not know why he was running or where.

"Can I help make your new spear?" he asked me now.

"I need chert from my father-in-law," I said. "We must think of a good trade."

Ali was proud to tell me the news of camp. Crane had finished sewing a winter parka for Vole. Dipper wept when she broke an ivory comb. Also, the pride of lions who shared our summer grounds had come to hunt near us, by the river. We had an agreement with this pride, led by a male marked by a jagged scar on his back. We avoided the lions' favorite resting areas and they avoided our noisy tents. In the mornings we waited past dawn to get water, and we never went to the river after sunset. On their part, the lions drank and killed at night.

I thought of the two males we had seen on the mammoth hunt. If they followed us here and defeated the leader, they would destroy the young cubs and upset the lionesses. It was a good time to be careful.

For that reason, the next morning Tit and Vole decided not to fetch the meat we had cached. I did not mind, for I had eaten my fill. But some of the other women were annoyed.

In our camp, Dipper was a woman who often complained. If she had peccary meat, she wanted antelope. If she had antelope, she wanted mammoth. One evening as clouds turned red over the long hills, Dipper spilled a gourd of water. It was too late to send a child to the river, and now she had to borrow from my sister, Sage. Dipper grumbled although Sage was generous.

When the first stars appeared in Old Woman's sky, Ali came to me. "I cannot find Chi." My daughter looked guilty. "I think he went to get our aunt more water."

I put down my pot of pitch. This was the second coat for the sinews that wrapped the spear point to its haft.

"He wanted to help make this spear," I replied, confused by what Ali was saying.

"I have looked everywhere, and one of our gourds is missing." Her voice went up, too shrill for a girl. "He does not think the lions will hurt him, because of Father, because he thinks he also has a lion under his skin."

"So?" I asked. "Why would a lion care about that?"

Ali's face wavered like the reflection in a pond.

The hills were black now, the sky brushed by turquoise in the west. I went to my own father to get his spear.

"I am well now," Father said. "I will go with you."

Etol and Wolf joined us at the central fire. The tall shapes of our tents rose up on either side. Their bulky darkness seemed solid and comforting.

"When we find Chi at the river," Etol spoke, "I will make him wish he had seen lions instead."

Gratefully I nodded. I also felt angry—for a boy to put us all in danger! My fear and anger made me sick.

"Should I bring a torch?" Wolf asked.

"Yes, you and Willow," my father agreed. "But stay behind me. The light weakens my eyes."

We felt our way down the side of the bluff, along the path to the river. I longed for moonrise and kept my torch low, trying to stretch my eyes into the trees. I saw Chi coming toward us, uncomfortable and ashamed. I saw him lying by a rock, his head bloody. I saw a lioness dragging him into the bushes, his thin legs bumping up from the ground. I saw his body half eaten as I have seen many bodies eaten with their stomachs open and muscles torn out in chunks. I pushed down a cry and stumbled against Etol.

"Ung," he grunted.

My father stopped, braced against the slope.

"What?" Wolf hissed.

We were all nervous, unable to see.

"Should we call out?" I asked.

"No," my father said. "And stop walking like a bear."

Now we went more slowly down the path, so familiar in the day.

"I'll teach him a good lesson," Etol whispered to comfort me.

It seemed I could hear Chi crying. At first I heard it inside my body, a weeping that pushed aside my lungs. Soon my father heard it too and sprinted ahead. From the sound of water I knew we were very close to the river. The rest of us also hurried down the path, looking for the shine of an animal's eye.

There it was, one gleam, two.

Wolf raised his torch of pitched pine and I did the same, thrusting the light in front of me. Dimly we could see two sleek bodies, two small lionesses hunting together. One dragged Chi into a bush while the other stood nearby as though looking on, willing to wait her turn. Clearly these lions were not hungry. Likely this was a second meal and they were hunting for practice more than need.

When they smelled the torches, they turned to face us, their back hairs rising so that they looked bigger.

My father planted his feet, yelled, and aimed his spear. Etol joined him. Wolf also shouted at the lions, hoping to frighten them from their meat.

These lionesses were young and our scent strange to them, especially the smoke from the pitched pine. The female holding Chi dropped him to snarl, showing her teeth. The other female also crouched and growled, a low furious rolling sound.

Encouraged, my father, Etol, and Wolf yelled again and shook their spears. I held my torch so tightly, I bruised my palm. I also raised my spear over my shoulder, but my throat had closed and I could only moan, a pitiful sound. My thoughts had fled into Chi's body. The bloody breath of the hunter covered my face.

Surprisingly my father began to speak, his voice stern.

"This is our child," he said to the lionesses. "You are not so hungry. Leave that child here. We will not return to the river at night. Leave that child."

My father was careful not to insult the lions. Still he spoke as a leader, fearlessly, and my strength returned. Once again I knew who I was. I sent out from my eyes and skin a strong feeling of determination. I glared into the face of the animal growling over my son. From deep in my chest I began to growl too. I would have stepped forward, but Etol touched me warningly on the wrist.

The lions took a moment to decide.

Then silently the second lioness disappeared.

That left the female guarding Chi. She showed her yel-
low teeth and hissed. The sound softened my knees. Even so I stood ready.

Suddenly the lion's hindquarters relaxed and lowered as though she were about to sit and wash herself. In a shift of mood, her slanted eyes blinked and she looked puzzled—that smell? that smoke?—before she also disappeared in the darkness.

Of course, we were not out of danger. Other members of the pride might be hunting here tonight, and these two might easily return. I picked up Chi, wanting to hold him hard against my breast, to squeeze his flesh into mine. Instead I was gentle, for I felt the wetness of his blood on my arm. In the torchlight, one side of his face looked dark where the lioness had struck his head. A more experienced hunter would have followed with a killing bite before dragging the body into cover. I held my son, unbelieving.

My father led us home, as fast as we could go along the dark path, breathing heavily up the bluff. When we came to the central fire, everyone stood there, my uncle, Golden, Vole, Tit, Bram, Dipper, Crane, Sage, crowding around us. I gave Chi to my aunt. My mouth was dry.

"Please," I said to her.

Days passed before we knew if Chi would recover. All

that night he did not open his eyes, and for two nights after he did not speak. I worried most about the blow to his head. My aunt, our healer, worried about the fever and kept Chi's bitten shoulder covered with a poultice of herbs. The muscles there were so badly torn that I wept tears for the first time. Men who do not hunt can be useful, but they are not often happy.

One morning we saw that Chi was still himself and that his shoulder wounds were healing a healthy yellow-brown. Shyly he asked for food and for the story of his rescue from the lion's mouth. I think he had already heard this story, for everyone in the camp knew it well. My father told it once before the central fire, repeating exactly what he had said to the lionesses. Then his sons and grandchildren retold that at their fires, adding any details they could imagine.

It *had* been a proud moment—four people, at night, against two hunting lions! My father regained something he lost when the stallion kicked him. My uncle was jealous but hid it well. Wolf preened. Etol was just as bad.

I spent most of my time tending Chi, not listening to my relatives shape this into a boast for the next spring gathering. My role in the story would not be a good one. I was the mother of the child who had put four hunters in danger. No one wanted to reproach me yet. But that would come.

Finally it was Dipper, speaking before all the women as we bathed in the cold water of the river. Winter was near, when we would bathe less often.

"How is your son?" my cousin asked.

My teeth chattered. "Better," I said glumly.

"I hope he has learned." Dipper was solemn. "I hope he understands what he has done."

My cousin stared at me, straight and tall in the weak sunshine as the shallows of the river surged around her legs. The cold did not seem to bother her. She was vain, proud of her body and always happy to see it without clothes.

I held back my first reply. At least she had waited until Chi was well, sitting in his bed, restless and whining. Secretly I wanted to blame Dipper. It was she, after all, who had taken Sage's water after spilling her own. My son had only gone to help his aunt. This all started with Dipper's carelessness.

"I think he understands," I said only. "It will be a bitter lesson if he never hunts."

Now my cousin looked guilty, staring down at the water. Her sons had grown up playing with mine. We ourselves, Dipper and I, had played together, building tiny tents out of animal scraps, childhood games where I brought home the meat and she cooked it. Dipper did not want to see Chi harmed.

Impulsively she came close and took my hand. "I am sure he will be fine," she said with strong emotion. "My mother is a good healer."

I dressed as fast as I could, like a young girl, anxious and shy. Dipper's kindness made me feel guilty too.

There were reasons for that.

Chapter Three

I have seen the mammoths court and mate. A male mammoth in rut can make a woman laugh but never a man. The shaggy male dribbles urine as he walks so that his inner thighs become black and wet. His penis is hugely swollen like an awkward fifth leg. On each side of his face, the glands also swell and drip a slimy liquid. He carries his head high, his chin tucked in. When he enters a family group, he goes from female to female, touching their vulvas with the tip of his trunk, tasting for someone ready to breed.

If the bull does not want to alarm the other mammoths, he will approach them slowly with his trunk draped casually over one tusk. The females are anxious and interested. His sharp smell fascinates even the younger calves. They hurry toward the stranger while their mothers and older sisters hesitate, come forward, urinate, rumble, and swing their feet.

Now an experienced female will attract the male by walking quickly away, her ears lifted, her head half turned to look behind her. If the bull is too young or too old, she will run as fast as she can, and the bull will lose the chase. If the bull is attractive, she will run clumsily and be caught.

I have seen Red Fur run clumsily across the plain and be caught by a bull twice her size. His tusks were enormous, swooping and curving. When she stopped, he moved his trunk to the top of her head and rested for a moment. Then he reared up, front feet on her hindquarters, his weight on his back legs. Covered in green slime, his penis hardened into the shape of a snake winding in the sand. This penis was as long as Chi and could move on its own, whipping back and forth until it found the opening in Red Fur's vulva. As Red Fur moved in closer, the bull balanced heavily. They stood like that, completely still.

When the bull withdrew, Red Fur bellowed. At this, her mother and grown children came rushing over, trumpeting, screaming, flapping their ears. They crowded around the couple, as excited as if they had just mated themselves! Red Fur would stay with this bull another three or four days, and they would mate another three or four times, always to the great interest of her family. One morning, Red Fur would lose interest. Her cycle was over. Still in rut, the bull would go looking for another female.

During the difficult time when Chi was in my tent, healing from the lionesses' attack, Etol and I met in secret outside camp. We mated quickly because it was cold and we were nervous. Etol grinned and showed his white teeth, full of desire. I enjoyed the feeling of a man inside me.

But even as we climaxed and held each other, we listened for footsteps or the sound of a voice. I imagined Dipper with her gathering basket crashing through the rabbitbrush. Etol told me, half joking, that he feared his sister, Crane, more. For the first time I learned how much my brother's wife disliked me.

"Because you hunt the mammoth," Etol explained. "Crane

wanted to do that when she was small, but she was not a strong hunter, and our father said no."

I breathed in the smell of Etol's chest. Four black hairs decorated the skin around his nipple. "I am going to put my shirt on now," he teased me. "I wish we could be inside, Willow, in my tent."

After our second time, Etol wanted to go to my father and arrange our marriage. "I have part of a mammoth tusk," he said, "that Dipper is carving into an animal. I can promise more. I could kill a bear this winter."

I spoke without thinking. "I do not want to be your second wife."

Etol looked surprised and angry. "What do you want, then?"

I hurried to put on my clothes. "Just this." I shrugged at where we had lain on the fallen leaves of a red oak tree. Bits of leaf and dirt were still in his hair and in mine.

Etol replied scornfully. "How often can we meet here alone, unnoticed? We cannot even hunt together without Golden or Wolf. Do you think Dipper doesn't suspect?"

Now I felt like a bird in a snare. "Do you think," I said nastily, "that Dipper will be happy carving a tusk so you can marry a second wife?"

We parted with the argument between us. But Etol could never stay angry long, not like Jak, who banked his fires and tended his grudges. The next time I lay with Dipper's husband, the red leaves fell again from our hair.

"How is Chi?" he asked while we dressed.

"Horrible, complaining." I spoke lightly. In fact, Chi worried me until I wanted to run away and forget him—as I did forget him for these few moments. Chi could not do much if he could not hunt. He had never shown any skill in carving ivory or working stone. I did not see him as a shaman or a storyteller. If the muscles in his shoulder did not heal, he would die of uselessness. That is what I thought.

"Chi is young enough to accept me as a father," Etol said, as I knew he would.

"No." I shook my head, amused. "He is not. You talk about this every time, always after, not before."

"Dipper knows about us." Etol put on his parka, the gray wolf fur circling his face. "Why do you look surprised? I could not keep lying to her, the mother of my children. And I am tired of being cold."

My own shock made me forget the cold. Now before my eyes, large white flakes appeared in the air, drifting and tumbling, swirling in the wind. What had happened to me that I had not seen these clouds, this snow coming?

"It is almost winter," Etol said. "This way, under the trees, is over. Our family will not allow this to go on. Your father will accept my gifts, and he will give something to my father, and we can mate in my tent."

Picking up his spear, Etol moved away, confident I would follow.

My husband's brother was right to talk to me as though I were a child. It had been foolish to think I could lie with a man so simply, without consequence. He was also foolish if he thought this matter would end easily for him, without regret. Neither of us expected the anger we met when we returned to camp.

Most of that fell on my head, as painful as blows. This was not only about Etol and me. The people were still upset by Chi's thoughtless trip to the river. My son had broken our agreement with the lions. Now one of those lions had tasted human blood. My son had endangered four hunters. Now he himself might become a burden.

"You have watched the mammoths instead of watching your children." Crane spoke in front of the adults at the central fire. The young ones had already been sent to the tents, where they strained to hear as much as they could. "Chi and Ali are too bold," Crane said. "They cannot be controlled."

My sister, Sage, exhaled so that everyone would hear. "*I* have watched these children," she said, outraged. "How dare you criticize them? We are here to talk about Willow and Etol!"

"Wait," my father interrupted. "I agree we must discuss the boy. But how can you complain about my granddaughter? She is almost a woman. She is a hard worker!"

Now my aunt spoke up for Chi, her dead sister's grandson. "Chi is like his father, Jak." My aunt looked at Bram, my father-in-law, waiting for his support.

"Boys can be too bold," Bram said immediately. "When they are older and more mature, these boys make the best hunters. My son Jak," Bram reminded us, "helped this family kill many mammoths."

"Perhaps it is hard," I said, "for a woman who has no son to understand." This was aimed at Crane, who had three daughters. "Jak died hunting for this family. I have tried to be a good parent to my son. I went with the mammoth hunters to make my son proud and to give my children marriage gifts. Is that wrong?"

My uncle answered now. "No one says it is wrong, Willow. We are happy Chi is safe. We are proud Ali is industrious. Your children help make this group strong, as do all our children."

His words made me calm down a little. This was the truth. Crane nodded reluctantly, and I nodded too.

"But we cannot be strong with so many secrets," my uncle continued. "Etol wants you as a second wife, and you must say yes or no. You can not have him *out* of camp if you will not have him *in* camp."

He gestured with his hand, once, twice. The crude joke heated my face.

I will say no, I decided.

But Dipper spoke first. "She must say yes!"

Dipper's face was swollen from crying, her black eyes hidden by rolls of flesh. "They have already been together," Dipper sobbed. "I would be ashamed if she did not become his second wife. How could we live in the same camp? What would I think every time they went hunting? She must live with us and share him where I can see it!"

My aunt and uncle looked embarrassed for their daughter. Etol frowned into the fire. Dipper liked this kind of excitement. Always she wanted to make things bigger and more important than they were. I saw a life filled with her tears and emotions.

"I will not," I said more bravely than I felt.

"This isn't good." My father shook his head.

Suddenly Vole spoke. "You had brothers who would help with your children's marriage."

As usual, my brother had followed his own thoughts. Now he was behind the rest of us. Vole stared at me with his small spiteful eyes. "You did not need to hunt for ivory. Ivory is not the only marriage gift. You should have stayed home, helping our father recover in his tent, instead of leaving that work to Crane."

For as long as I can remember, I have struggled with my older brother, Vole. He disliked me, I think, from the moment I replaced him at our mother's breast. He was three years old. Most children wean naturally. Vole fought for that breast the rest of his life.

In this way, at the central fire, we made our alliances. In the coming days I would find my sister Sage, my brother Wolf, and my aunt unwillingly on my side. Vole, Tit, and Crane supported Dipper. My cousin Golden, my father-in-law Bram, and my own father murmured unhappily. They hated to offend any of their family and so ended up offending us all. My uncle remained calm and uninterested. He cared only for mammoth hunting. The children went on as usual, playing their games and begging for treats.

Etol did not know if he was angrier at me or at Dipper.

When it came time to sleep, he lay down by the central fire. Eventually people began to think he was more guilty than I was. Why, after all, did I not want to marry him? Perhaps he had forced me in some way? Why had he not controlled himself? Why could he not control me or his wife?

This quarrel was creating many problems. Soon we would all move to another valley, our winter camp, where we would repair the lodge that jutted from the mouth of a large cave. If the winter was long and cold, we would stay together in that lodge, sharing the same warmth and shelter through the storms. In summer, we change camps and move often. In winter, people grow irritable. It is a difficult season. No one wanted to start the cold months with these bad feelings.

At last my uncle talked with Etol, who came to stand outside the flap of my tent. His voice was pleasant. I invited him in. Sitting cross-legged before the fire, in front of my children, Etol spoke frankly. Chi knew of his disgrace and for once was silent. Ali kept her face turned down.

"We must solve this problem," my brother-in-law began. His hands rested on his thighs, politely, as though he and I were strangers. "It has always made sense that you become my second wife. I am the only man here for you except my father, Bram, who is too old. You were my brother's wife. These are my brother's children. They should become my children."

Etol lifted his hand to stop me from speaking. "Also I care about you. And I would be a good husband. I have shown you that."

Now he grinned, his white teeth showing.

I glanced at Chi, whose expression did not change. My son did not understand his uncle's meaning. But Ali ducked her head even lower.

Etol paid them no attention. "You do not want to live with your cousin Dipper." Etol grimaced. For now, at least, he did not want to live with Dipper either. "If you will move your tent closer to mine, you can stay there, in your own tent as my second wife. In the winter lodge, you must also stay close to me and my family. In time, your thoughts will change. You will want to be with us."

Looking straight at me, Chi shook his head.

I also did not like this idea. Yet I had to wonder—could I say no? Golden and Sage might support me, but my aunt would not. Everyone in the camp wanted a solution. Everyone hoped we would settle this soon.

I warned Chi with my eyes.

"What does Dipper say?" I asked, curious.

"Your aunt, her mother, talks to Dipper every day." Etol spoke dryly. "Dipper will do what her husband tells her."

Ali looked up and we exchanged a smile.

That is how I married for the second time, with a gift giving that brought all my family together. Even Dipper gave me a bundle of herbs to strengthen a woman's blood. She must have expected this marriage as soon as Jak died, for she almost looked relieved. To my father, Etol gave an ivory carved by Dipper into the shape of a cheetah. My father promised Bram four skins, which I would have to tan. My stepchildren, two boys and a girl, gave me blue stones, and I gave each one a blue feather.

Although Chi's scars were hidden by his shirt, I could see that he felt uncomfortable, so soon from his bed, surrounded by people. Fortunately no one felt like singing and no one started to dance. The gift giving was short. When it was over, I went back to my tent.

That was a bad winter for me, not cold but strange and very windy. For weeks at a time we lived in the lodge, where a fire always burned to heat the walls of the cave. This cave had to be cleaned thoroughly with handfuls of sweet grass, for foxes lived here in our absence. Protected from the storms, five adults and a few children could sleep comfortably in the inner room. On its rocky ledges, we also stored tools, hides, and baskets of food. Each year, from the mouth of the cave, we built another room of poles thatched with branches, covered in animal skins, and chinked with mud. Many mammoth tusks strengthened the roof, making it tall enough for us to stand up and stretch our arms. Sometimes we could hear animals walking above us, stopping at the smoke hole and sniffing.

In a long winter my family has to work hard bringing in enough wood for the fire and hunting meat so that we can keep working hard. At the front of the lodge was a door into which we all crawled on our hands and knees. Here it was colder but less smoky, and here I lived near Etol and Dipper and their three children. By now, Dipper's youngest son was past weaning, a sweet boy who had begun to make his first tiny spear.

When Dipper and I discovered we were pregnant, the news made Etol boast. Look at all the children he would have! We hushed him quickly, speaking together in irritation. The children were not born yet.

Etol must have felt a shift in the wind. It was our right now, and for some years, to refuse mating. He suddenly looked less happy. Over the body of a coyote, Dipper and I worked side by side. We skinned it fast, wanting the meat. I put my cold hands in the animal's warm chest.

"You can have your husband now," I whispered to Dipper.

"Oh no, you can have him." She giggled back.

Laughter is one way to live in the lodge. Dipper and I made our truce with laughter, and the men made so many jokes about Etol's penis that he also laughed and put aside his desire at night. The adults sang song after song with the children, and my aunt told funny stories as well as serious ones. We did not really feel so cheerful, but it was wise to pretend. The winter always starts with this kind of humor. We hope, by spring, we will still be speaking to each other.

As I have before, I made a vow never to become pregnant again. I craved to be in the fresh air, surrounded by snow that had just fallen, but when I put on my winter clothes and took up my spear and went outside, I only felt deeply tired. Then I craved to be back in the lodge, sleeping under my bearskin. Still I had to gather firewood and help carry the meat that the hunters brought home. I talked little with

Chi or Ali, who spent most of their time near my sister, Sage. My jokes with Dipper faded. As much as possible, I stayed under that bearskin.

One night, as the wind tore at the roof of our lodge, I dreamed of the shaggy mammoths in summer. Old Man shone yellow-white in a blue sky. The smell of sweet tall grass filled my nostrils, and I widened them to bring that smell down into my lungs. Strangely, none of the mammoths could see or hear me, and I stood close, unnoticed, to one young female who knelt on her back legs. Now she stretched her front legs forward and rocked back and forth. She rocked, heaved up, walked a few steps, knelt on her back legs, and rose again. She was waiting for the birth of her first child.

After a long time, the mammoth simply lay on her side, panting in distress. Two members of her family group left their grazing to stand beside her. The matriarch of the herd, Half Ear, rumbled low. Then she used her tusk to poke the female hard in the rump. The pregnant mammoth struggled to her feet and began once more to back up, kneel, and stretch out her legs. Whenever she tried to lie down, the matriarch poked her unsympathetically. Red Fur also stayed close by, grumbling and flapping her ears.

Finally the female stood and swayed with her head hanging, her glands streaming liquid. In a rush of blood, a bulge appeared below her tail. Groaning, near the end of her strength, the mammoth knelt, stretched, and rocked. Out of the bulge, a calf slithered to the ground, where it lay motionless. Using their trunks, Red Fur and Half Ear tore the placenta and tried to get the newborn to his feet. The baby did not move.

Red blood, the color of poppies, poured from the mother's vulva, pooling in the dirt, snaking through the grass. She trembled violently and sank to her knees. Now Red Fur and Half Ear hurried to hold her up. One on each side, the three of them stumbled forward, leaving the dead baby behind. Suddenly the female fell, smashing her forehead before slipping sideways.

Interested, a circle of adolescent males and females began to surround the mother. Red Fur knelt and worked the front end of her tusks under the mammoth's shoulder. Grunting, she began to lift so that she carried the full weight of the female's front quarters.

Crack! A sound like thunder startled us all. The circle of mammoths jumped, jostling and squeaking. One of Red Fur's tusks had broken in half. Shaking her head in pain, Red Fur stumbled away, and the dying mammoth fell again to the earth.

A long afternoon passed before she stopped breathing. Red Fur and Half Ear never left her side, while other members of the group came by to touch her body and smell the blood. I thought I heard that blood talking to me, and I crouched closer in the grass to listen.

After this dream, many months later, I saw the matriarch and her herd grazing on a yellow field between the long-needled pines. One of Red Fur's tusks was broken in half. I knew then that my dream had slipped through the wind of that winter night into the future.

Thankfully, it was not my future.

That same summer, as the female gave birth to her first child and died, I gave birth to my third child and lived. My daughter Crow came easily after a morning of painful cramps. Ali and Sage held a willow basket for the placenta. They brought moss for the blood and other fluids. My baby's wrists and ankles were rolled with fat. Ali's face split into a smile that hid her black eyes. Proudly she put her sister on my stomach.

In a few days Dipper also had a healthy son, and our family celebrated with a dance under the moonless face of Old Woman. Dazed, I watched Etol stamp his feet and twirl around the central fire. Behind him stood a row of racks for stretching hides. I thought about making my husband new shoes, from a buffalo robe, with the hair turned in. When I grew sleepy, I went back to my tent, my daughter sucking fiercely, my heart as open as the petals of a flower.

Slowly, slowly, my baby's head tipped and her mouth eased away from the dark nipple. White milk puddled on her perfect lips. The bearskin sighed as we cuddled under it. I also had children, the skin whispered. Two sweet cubs. Shall I tell you that story?

Chapter Four

Like you, I believe that everything changes and nothing goes away. I covered my husband Jak with red ochre and buried him by the roots of an oak tree. Bit by bit, beetles and worms took his flesh and he began to live that life, in the darkness, moving through soil. His bones remain entwined with the roots of the oak and send their thoughts through sap to the green leaves growing in spring. The flint of his spear remembers cliffs that are far away. The sinews that bind the flint remember running with the deer herd, the press of haunches on a cold morning. The mammoth tusk—if I had given him that tusk!—would remember its life as a favorite son of the matriarch. Jak's bones remember their own life, a hunter, a father, a husband. They rest comfortably in the earth.

I think of Jak's inside animal, the lion spirit under his skin. That part of him returned long ago to the lions. It curls in a rough tongue licking fur. My son, Chi, thought his father's spirit would watch over him. Now Chi knows better, for he has felt that lion bite into his shoulder.

I think some animals have the spirits of people under their skin. I have seen the raccoon who looks too curiously and the bear who knows all our tricks.

Like you, I believe that nothing goes away and everything is important. My flesh in the earth will show me the importance of soil as I am carried into the darkness, bit by bit, to live that life.

When I hunted on the plain, under the pink and red of Old Man's sky, it was only important how I made the morning fire. Carefully I put down my tinder and fed in the smaller sticks and twigs, watching the coals catch and burn orange. My hands had never been so cold. The dead fire came alive. I had never been so grateful.

My uncle sickened in the winter and we could not leave him. So we missed the next gathering. When my father's brother finally died, we buried him with piles of ivory selected from many different mammoths. Their stories would entertain him for a long time. My uncle had lived to see his grandchildren, and we count that a good life. Now one of his grandchildren, Dipper's girl, was ready to mate and have a child of her own. So was my daughter Ali. My brother Wolf and cousins Tit and Golden were also impatient to find wives. Two springs later, my group made sure we were among those camped by the big river under the narrow-leafed trees.

My youngest daughter was not yet three. Etol named her Crow because of the black hair that flapped like two wings on each side of her head. He named his third son Second Crow because the little boy was always behind his half sister, both of them jabbering so that they sounded like a flock of birds. They were beautiful babies, Crow and Second Crow, fat and stubborn and busy. Even after they learned to speak like human beings, they kept their secret language, which they whispered to each other late in the night, heads together.

"Sleep now! Be quiet!" Dipper would yell. She treated

Crow like one of her own, just as Second Crow was also mine. Many nights he stayed in my tent. As often, Crow went with him and I was alone again with Ali and Chi.

Like the other boys, Chi hunted small game. The muscles in his shoulder had finally healed, although the scars were painful when he bent his arm too far. The lioness bit him again every time he threw his spear, and for this reason he threw it awkwardly. Etol wondered if Chi would ever throw the heavier weapon needed for mammoths. I knew that hunters like Tit and Vole distrusted my son. There is more to hunting than a strong arm, and Chi was sullen, angry at certain animals, angry at his weakness. Sage and I talked about him many times.

"He is like Jak," Sage said.

It was bitter to see the man in the boy. Once Jak had beaten me, something I remembered well.

"He should be more like his grandfather," Sage continued. "Bram is a good man, a fair hunter, no one to be ashamed of."

I did not say the obvious to my sister. Bram was liked—but not much respected among the men. Chi had no desire to be more like his grandfather.

In my tent there was one person who never surprised me. As my father boasted, Ali had become a hard worker, skilled with plants, patient with children. For nearly two years she had had her monthly blood. At this spring gathering I hoped to find her a good match, someone we could welcome into our family group. In a bundle of deerskin, wrapped in moss, I kept a necklace of beads from the ivory I got on my first hunt. I could also offer some furs and tanned skins. Ali herself had a full set of tools, baskets and fishing nets, awls and needles, wooden bowls and spoons. She would give these as well if she wanted a husband.

That year the gathering happened far down the big river, farther south than I had ever been, but familiar to my old aunt. We knew of the time and place from meeting some hunters at the edge of our winter grounds. After walking fast for three days, we arrived early and chose the campsite with the best view. Protected under the giant narrow-leafed trees, we looked out over a brown river so large, no one in my family had ever crossed it.

Another group joined us, keeping a polite space between our central fire and theirs. A noisy bunch came next, with lots of children, who cut down a forest of saplings to build themselves shelters. The fourth family was also big and camped on our other side, so that we could smell the peccary they roasted that afternoon. The last family stayed far from the river, apart from everyone.

The eye of Old Woman grew as wide as it could, eager to stare down on our dancing. This was not a large gathering and not a small one. I felt content and anxious all at once.

The eye of Old Woman is said to be many things. It hangs above us like a nut or piece of fruit. As we watch the moon change, we are comforted by changes that are always the same. We admire its beauty. We can look into Old Woman's eye, and she can look back.

The eye of Old Man gives us heat and light. Without the sun, we would clearly die.

But what does the moon do? Endlessly we wonder.

At our gatherings we dance under the face of Old Woman and celebrate our journey to this land. First of all the men form a circle around a blazing fire and stamp their feet while the women slap their thighs. Then all the women form a circle around the fire and stamp their feet while the men slap their thighs. We do this only in a gathering. In our own families, men and women naturally dance together. A gathering often divides us in this way, men against women, one family against another. A gathering can be dangerous, for it is not easy to act properly with people you do not know.

When I was young, I did not understand why the men and women had to separate or why the children were discouraged from dancing. As I grew older, I saw that this was the time to see all in a row the marriageable men and the marriageable women. The mothers of daughters watch this circle of future sons-in-law carefully. The daughters also stare and make judgments as the men dance, young and old, one next to the other, their genitals flapping. When the women dance and the men slap their thighs, it is the men's turn to compare and plan. I saw then why this celebration was under Old Woman, in praise of the night, the nights in our tents, the mating of men and women, the birth of children.

At this gathering, I was one of those mothers who watched coldly as the men circled the fire. In the other four families who came that spring, there were seven hunters not yet married. Three of these were the grandchildren of my mother's oldest brother, too close to my lineage. One had a limp, and I thought of Chi. Still I did not want this man for my daughter. I rejected another because he danced wildly, like Jak had danced long ago. That left two sons from parents I knew fairly well. Their group lived close to our winter lodge. The woman was good at working stone, and the father still hunted mammoths and buffalo. One boy was older than Ali, the second younger. Each appeared to be strong and well behaved.

The more I watched them, the happier I became. If Dipper's daughter also took one of these boys, both families would be pleased. Brothers hunt well together. Secretly I had dreaded this gathering and the changes it might bring. But now a son-in-law suddenly seemed desirable. A son-in-law meant grandchildren. My heart beat faster to the beat of the drum. Grandchildren meant danger for Ali, her first child and the most difficult birth. I put that unlucky thought aside. Impatiently my feet tapped the ground. I was eager for my turn to dance.

At this gathering we had a drum from the family who camped alone, away from the river. One of their men was a shaman with long hair that hung unbraided. He beat the rhythm to the dance, his hair a darkness around his shoulders, and he danced too, grinning like a boy in heat. My uncle had told stories of shamans. We knew of their willingness to trance and talk to Old Woman, and we were eager to see this happen. The shaman's group came from far away and spoke our language comically, slurring some words, barking others. Still they had ties to another family here, for the shaman's wife claimed that lineage.

Along with our prayers, sparks from the fire flew up into the sky. We added buffalo fat, and this smell completed the song we were making with our feet, the song of the circle, the song of the greasy fat, the song of the flames. Finally the shaman put down his drum and began to whirl, not around the fire but in a circle all his own.

His thick black hair covered his face so that he looked like a bear, shaggy and big. His hands curved into his chest like paws. A growling noise came from the cloud around his shoulders. Sometimes we caught a glimpse of bared teeth and eyes rolled up white. I became alarmed. This man's spirit was the giant short-faced bear, able to kill a lion, willing to kill anything. Black bears and cave bears eat plants and grubs. The short-faced bear will eat only meat.

I wondered if Old Woman would talk to this creature. No one but the shaman was dancing now. He became our fire, and we circled around him. When his eyes glowed, we all moved back. I looked for Chi, standing next to Etol. Crow and Second Crow were asleep in my tent. I reached for Ali's hand. White bubbles frothed from the shaman's mouth. His growls scared the dogs one family had brought. Soon the howls of these dogs blended with the roars of the bear.

The shaman reached up to the eye of Old Woman. His long black hair became a pelt and I saw him grow tall, reaching up his hands, twice as tall as my father, towering above me with his claws curved in, his red mouth wide.

The bear rose and scratched at the night. Old Woman laughed as she batted him down, a lioness slapping a cub. The shaman crumpled and lay in the dirt, his body limp, his eyes closed. Tomorrow he would tell us what he saw. For now the dance was over.

Carelessly the shaman's wife and two of his brothers picked him up and carried him away. Although the shaman's thick hair still swept the ground, the rest of him seemed small and shrunken. He looked like a child being put to bed.

"Mother," Ali protested, for I still squeezed her hand.

"Did you see those two boys from the woman with flint under her skin?" I asked. I wanted to shake away that vision of the bear growing tall. I remembered a bobcat I had once seen, shaking off water, its nose wrinkled. "Which is your favorite?"

Ali shrugged irritably. Her hand was sweaty. "Perhaps the oldest," she said. "I don't know."

I understood her confusion. So many strangers, so many possibilities! I knew that her thoughts were dizzy, her mouth dry. Tonight she would not sleep but gossip with the other girls her age, unmarried women she had just met at the river or by the fire. Touching each other, they would compare tattoos and the ritual of first blood, exchanging the stories of their lives. They would think they were learning more at this gathering than in all their years with their parents.

Ali went away, into the night, and I made my plans. The next morning I went to find my father. I wanted him to speak to the woman who works stone. My father was skillful in this way. He would know how to tell a mother why she should give up two sons.

In the group camped near ours, I saw the men of my family eating antelope with the men of that family. My brother Vole told the story of Father's speech to the lioness.

Boldly he mimicked my father's words. "Give us that child," he scolded. "You are not so hungry. That child is ours."

One man scoffed, "I have never heard of people taking meat from lions."

An old man protested. "Is this a story or the truth?"

This man's teeth were so worn that a boy sat next to him chewing meat, which he put half eaten on the old man's thigh.

"Chi," Vole ordered. "Lift up your shirt."

My son's face stiffened, and I could almost see the start of a pout, how his lips would push out as they did when he was young. But Chi was nearly grown now, and he did not want to shame his uncle. Slowly he stood and lifted his leather shirt so the men could see the scars on his shoulder.

"Wah!" a man said. "That is a lion's bite. I have seen one before. But the girl died."

In small movements I tried to signal my father. Chi saw me and scowled, quickly covering his chest. With a graceful wave, Etol came over to stand by my side. These were hunting stories, boasts and brags. None of the men wanted me here. I knew I would have to talk to Father later.

For now I would get Etol's support. I wanted the older boy for Ali, but Etol and Dipper needed to approach the parents for the younger son. It would be best if we went together.

Gatherings do not last long. We would not see the round eye of Old Woman again, not under these trees, by this river. This place grew less beautiful every day as we used up the wood and gathered the good plants. Some people left their feces unburied, and the smell of so many humans attracted flies. Of course, the hunting was bad too.

So I planned and pushed, and the next morning my father went to the parents of these boys.

Dipper and Etol got ready their marriage gifts.

Golden and Tit spent most of their time in the shaman's camp, where two girls needed husbands. When no one came to talk with my aunt, she went with fresh meat to the girls' father, who explained that he waited for another man who would marry the sisters as a first and second wife. My aunt was offended. It caused bad feelings for some men to have two women and some to have none.

Many of us felt the strain of living so closely with new people. When my brother Wolf found no one to marry, he convinced Vole to go off hunting with him and some other young men. Vole and Crane had been arguing for days, loud enough for everyone to hear. Even the children in our camp began to fight with the children in other camps. We counted the time until we could go home.

At last the parents of those boys came to the small tent

my family shared with Sage and Bram. The woman praised my furs and the ivory necklace. She agreed to speak with enthusiasm to her sons.

That same afternoon Ali also came while I was nursing Crow. When the little girl saw her sister, she pushed away my nipple and put out her hands.

"Take me to get berries," Crow begged.

Ali smiled down at her. "I have some dried berries."

"No!" Crow shook her head. Her hair flapped like two black wings. "Juicy berries."

"Silly," I said, feeling grumpy. Crow was ready to wean, but I was not. I liked her little hands on my breasts. "There will be fresh berries when we return to the summer camp. And that is soon, greedy bird."

These last words were meant for Ali. I stood up, hoping to find some distraction for Crow.

"Where is Second Crow?" I wondered out loud. "Is he eating something with his mother?"

On her feet, my daughter flew away to find her half brother. Smiling too, I took Ali's arm, anxious to share all my good news. The two sons and their parents were willing. My father and I were pleased.

Ali's braids were even with mine. She had grown tall, with big hips and strong legs. A beautiful woman, I thought proudly before I noticed how her eyes turned to the side of my face. My daughter did not want to look at me. She had news of her own.

When I heard it, I dropped her arm and went back into the tent. I did not want anyone to see us now. After Ali followed, I closed the flap, my thoughts running, a jumble of words, stories, ideas. How could I prevent this? Struggling, I did not speak until I could control my voice.

Ali wanted to become the shaman's second wife. She had already spoken to him. Perhaps—I did not ask—they had even mated.

"Why?" I found a word to spit out.

Ali had a lot to say. "When I saw him trance, Mother, I knew then. His bear spirit looked at me, and I saw Old Woman reach down her hand and touch him, and I felt her hand sweep over me, and I felt strange. The next day we talked. He knows so much about plants and medicine. His wife knows even more! They can teach me so much, and they go to places where new plants grow. Their hunting grounds are far to the south, places I have never been."

I heard myself shouting. "What are you saying? You want to leave our camp? Daughters do not leave. You bring your husband to us!"

"Not always," Ali wept.

"Ali," I cried, "would you go with him?"

Yes, she would.

My sister did not try to console me. "She is my own daughter," Sage sobbed. "How could she?"

"She is like her mother, my sister-in-law," Crane said meanly.

My aunt slapped Crane hard on the cheek.

"This is a terrible loss." My aunt was stern. "Ali is a hard worker. We have lost her skills. We have lost the children she might have given our camp."

Dipper complained, "We have already talked to the parents of these boys. They wanted their sons to be together. We showed them our marriage gifts."

"Willow should say no to her daughter." Crane spoke angrily, holding her bruised face. "We can force Ali to return. We can tie her with yucca rope."

I wanted to hit this woman myself. How could Etol have such a sister? She saw my daughter with her hands tied!

"He is a shaman," my aunt reminded Crane coldly. "Do we want him as an enemy? Ali is a grown woman. Can we keep her against her will? Will you watch over her, day and night, hiding her from your new enemy the shaman?"

Things were happening too fast, out of our control. It is what we always fear at a gathering. The shaman and his group were leaving in a few days, and Ali was determined to go with them.

I moaned to Sage. "Nothing can move her."

My sister snapped, "Crane is right. Ali is like you. Hunting mammoths, living in your own tent, doing what you want to do."

I stared at my sister. Sage thought this? Almost I welcomed a new pain. I wanted to hurt more—or at least to hurt differently.

In the end I had to leave the gathering to calm myself, walking quickly, silently, away from our messy camp. The forest was dangerous with strange animals who made warning sounds in the bushes and grass. I did not know whose home I was entering. I was like a male lion traveling through new territory. In one clearing, I saw where black bears had ravaged all the plants and broken the oaks, pulling at anything that had fruits or nuts. I inspected the area. The damage was recent. At another meadow, I stopped where the pine trees had been rubbed smooth up to my shoulders, the inner wood yellow, polished, shiny. Heaps of buffalo wool lay on the ground.

In my thoughts, I saw Jak's bones. I prayed to them for the strength to put aside my grief. This seemed an odd thing to ask my first husband. But I wanted to say good-bye to my daughter, who was also his daughter. I needed his indifference. I needed his knowledge, turning to soil.

When Ali came the last time to our tent, my life broke in half. I broke open painfully so that half of me could enter my oldest child. She would leave with the shaman to new places, and I would never know what that other half of me saw or felt. I would never know what it was like to live with the spirit of the giant short-faced bear. I would never know if my daughter died giving birth or lived to nurse a boy or girl. Half of me would be gone. The half that remained would be blind and deaf.

"I will tell you everything at the next gathering," Ali chattered. "I have asked the shaman. He has agreed to come back."

I knew I would never see her again. Breaking in half was hard. But it was necessary.

"Take him your necklace," I said only. "Take him these furs."

When she lifted the flap, carrying her tools and marriage gifts, half of me walked to the shaman's camp and began our new life there. In this way we were still together, young and eager to be traveling south. Our desire burned away our loneliness.

The half that remained stayed in my tent for a long time. Crow came in to nurse, but I hardly noticed. When I felt her small hands, I tried to remember those other hands, those first caresses, and I could not. It had been too long ago. Now I could not bear Crow's touch. Everything changes and everything is important and Crow began to cry and Sage came to get her.

Soon Chi also sat beside me. The tent grew dark as the sun set behind the mountains west of the giant narrow-leafed trees. I could not see my son's face. I had no comfort for him either. Dimly I realized that someday Chi would also leave our camp. We say that men move easily. We expect our sons to go and our daughters to stay. My son would want a wife.

Impossibly, amazing myself, I began to think about Chi's marriage. With his scarred shoulder and sullen mouth, Chi was not an attractive mate. A match for him would need careful attention—and more gifts than usual.

My loneliness got bigger. I could not split in half for Chi. I could enter my daughter, but I could not enter my son. Perhaps, for that reason, I had loved him more.

As he often did, Chi knew my thoughts. "I will never leave you," he said in the darkness.

The next day I learned that Tit and Golden had also gone with the shaman's family. At the last possible moment, my aunt made an arrangement with the father of the two girls. I was glad that Ali would have relatives with her. But I felt new grief to part with my cousins, especially Golden.

My aunt looked terrible, her eyes red.

Our only consolation was the marriage of Dipper's daughter to the oldest boy of the woman with flint under her skin. In addition, the parents promised their younger son to Crane's oldest girl when she had her first blood. So closely tied, on the edge of our winter grounds, the parents hoped to see their sons often. On our part, we were glad to replace the two hunters we had lost.

A warm spring became a hot summer. Summer became fall, and the gathering was a memory in the winter lodge. Often I tried to see what the rest of me was doing, traveling south, sleeping with the shaman, sorting through plants with his first wife. I imagined myself happy learning new things. One day I saw myself pregnant. I saw a red rock in the sky. I saw a bear's claw covering the rock. I did not know what this meant.

Chapter Five

As Crow got older, I began to think about hunting again. I wanted to throw my spear at a mammoth and eat all I could from the fatty hump. I wanted more ivory for Chi. I felt dissatisfied with my first hunt. The male had run away to die. There was no reward in that.

Etol laughed pleasantly. He was a satisfied man lying in my tent after we mated. Crow was with Dipper. Chi pretended to sleep.

"You're not young anymore," my husband told me.

"You're not either."

"But I have been hunting all these years while you were with Crow. Also, at any time you could have another bird. I am not saying no. You should ask the other hunters."

"I will start with small game, deer and antelope."

"Sure," Etol grunted, turning on his side. This was his way, not to worry when there was no need. He knew my hands were weak. He knew I had stopped watching animals as closely as a hunter should. At any time too, I might start a child. Crow had not suckled since last fall, and it was spring again. Etol spent half his nights in my tent.

"Would you make me a throwing stick?" I asked him.

"It's too late for that," Etol said in his sleepy voice. "To use the atlatl, you must start early, as I did. Even Chi began when he was too old."

This disappointed me although I was not surprised. The atlatl would have increased the distance and force of my spear. Still, the throwing stick required more movement from the hunter, and this sometimes warned or startled an animal. It was also tricky to release the spear straight while holding on to the wooden shaft. Perhaps Etol was right. It was too late for me to learn this skill.

I heard Chi move in his bed. My son worked hard every day to use his atlatl. He was better than Etol would admit.

That night my dreams were boldly colored. A great fire blazed on the horizon, a line stretching east to west. The bad-tasting ground sloth told me she was thirsty. This sloth was small, about my size. Blinking and moist, her brown eyes looked into mine without fear. I felt ashamed, for I have used the sloth for target practice and I planned to do so soon again.

Next I was at the chert quarry, where we get our best points in orange rocks streaked with purple. Shorter than the mammoth, with tusks that grew out and not down, a female mastodon browsed in the gray-green thorny shrubs. Absurdly, a giant insect-eater tried to mate with her. Although the male insect-eater was the right size, his body was covered with a hard carapace, and he could not rise to mount.

"We are thirsty," the animals said. I agreed that these last years had been dry.

Now a herd of camels, creamy yellow, ran through my dream, trying to escape the fire that burned closer but gave no smoke. A dire wolf limped behind the herd, his ribs showing.

I forgot about that dream for years.

In camp, the next morning, my aunt asked me to find a certain plant good for digestion.

"I want to make a new spear," I said. I also had furs to tan and clothes to sew for Crow and Second Crow. In fact, I had many projects for many days ahead.

My aunt looked annoyed. "Could you find this plant if you wanted to?"

"Small red spots under the leaf." I spoke easily. "In a cool place, maybe under a log."

"Where would you go if I needed it now?"

I was silent.

"Ali would have known," my aunt said. "She would have seen that log the last time she went gathering. She would have a bag of these plants, dried, in her tent. Willow! You have let your daughter do what you needed to do. You used to have a good relationship with plants. What have they told you lately?"

This speech hurt my feelings. My aunt knew I did not like to talk about Ali. My family was not being kind. First Etol said I had spent too much time away from hunting. He said I was too old to use the throwing stick. Now my aunt said I had lost my relationship with plants. Perhaps no one in this camp thought I was good at anything.

Prudently I put my anger aside. My aunt was a leader, and I needed her support.

"If you want that plant, I will get it," I said loudly.

Dipper passed where we stood talking, her back bent by a bundle of wood. Behind her, Crow and Second Crow each carried an armful of sticks. Squinting sideways, my cousin looked at us.

My aunt nodded in a smug way. She tapped her bony finger on wrinkled lips. "Go to the black tree by the river," she advised. "And get some willow branches. I want you to make a basket."

My irritation rose again, like a fish coming up for flies.

Apparently I was expected to put aside my plans whenever my aunt thought I needed a lesson. Briefly I thought of saying no.

Instead I took with me the new hunter who had married Dipper's daughter. I liked to see him laugh when I made jokes about mating. Silently we walked down the path to the black tree, struck by lightning in the summer I gave birth to Crow. Under its dark branches, I put down my spear and found the red-spotted leaf growing in a hollow on the north side. Silently I filled my gathering basket. At a low place by the river, where the soil was wet, I cut the long new shoots of green willow. Stripping them of leaves, I piled them high in my pack.

"Is something wrong?" the new hunter asked.

He was a smart boy, careful to flatter all the men and win the approval of all the women. We congratulated ourselves on our good luck. Next year we would have his brother too!

"I have to make a willow basket," I said shortly, and turned without even studying the river. I hurried us back toward the bluff through the grassy meadow, past juniper and oak.

The husband of Dipper's daughter followed. "Do you dislike making baskets?" he finally dared.

His innocence made me smile and walk more slowly. The blue face of Old Man sat like a bowl over a land growing green and bright, green sweeps of grass, green leaves unwrinkling, green curls of fern, green cattail in the river, green mint in the shade of a quaking tree. The pines breathed their perfume into the air. Berries formed pink on the underside of bushes. I felt a kind of smiling all around, a faint humming. My aunt was right. I did not want to lose my good relationship with plants.

At my tent, I wrapped the willow branches in wet leaves and let them soften for three fingers of sky. Then with an obsidian flake, I cut the end of each branch, took one side of the butt between my teeth and swiftly pulled down the other side. The willow split in two, showing its white core, smelling of sap. Holding the butt, I tore off the bark in another quick motion. These branches were ripe and easy to prepare. I bit and pulled and soon had a pile of clean willow strips, beautiful to a woman about to make a basket.

Now I tied three branches and folded them back against each other in a round mat. With a bone awl, I made holes in the mat and sewed the branches together with more strips of willow. Slowly I let the base coil around and up so that the mat curved into the shape of a bowl like Old Man's sky. I wanted a large gathering basket. I wanted to impress my aunt.

My fingers could do this work alone, remembering how often they had slipped willow in and out, over and down. In this early spring, the flies had not yet hatched to invade our camp. Still the day was warm and the sun heated my skin, sinking deeper into my winter bones.

I felt proud knowing how much Old Man loved me, how much he loved my people. The clean white inside the willow flickered like the flanks of hills covered with flowers, like white milk puddling in a baby's mouth. The smell of willow rose fresh, sharp, tingling, and moist. My fingers moved delicately, trying to hear what was so faint.

In and out I worked the willow as Dipper and Crane went back and forth, preparing to gather roots from a field in the forest. They wanted me to help, but I shook my head.

"My aunt tells me to make a basket."

Dipper asked for the spears of Etol and Vole, and my fa- ther decided he would go with them.

Crow wanted to be with her grandfather. "Will there be berries?" she asked, hopping up and down.

"It's much too early," I told her, laughing. "And you are hopping like a flea."

"The berries will not be ripe for a month," Dipper said.

"Oh, I do not *think* so," Crow insisted, which made us all shake our heads.

Now Second Crow had to go as well, and Dipper sighed. "It will be a long walk," she warned him. "No one is carrying you!"

Crane took her middle girl to dig and pack roots.

"We are leaving behind these children." Crane gestured at her youngest daughter, whose dirty nose blew out a string of snot. Her oldest child stood by the drying racks filled with strips of horse and antelope. Every few minutes, she waved her arms listlessly, scaring away ravens.

"There are plenty of us here." I nodded at Crane.

In truth, Bram, Sage, and Wolf were at the river. Chi and Etol's sons hunted rabbits near the camp. My aunt slept soundly in her tent. That left only Dipper's daughter and new husband, who had both disappeared. Really, I would be the one watching Crane's children, my brother's children.

"Get me some fat tubers," I said to my sister-in-law. She owed me that now.

Willow loves water. My willow branches remembered the river flowing near their roots, flowing under them, moving away while they stayed behind, swaying gracefully. My branches were too young to know all the seasons of a willow's life, the clouds of insects in summer, the clacking of cicadas and high music of gnats. They had never felt the brush of lions against their bark or caught the hair of a jaguar or a muskrat come to drink.

Mostly my willows remembered their growth in this early spring—how quickly their shoots had flashed up from the soil, urged on by heat, urged on by light, bursting with juice, bursting with desire. Old Man loves us very much, the willows told me. Old Man calls and begs us to grow faster, faster, faster! We grow so fast that one day we will flower against the skin of the sky.

Sometimes I stopped my work when my nieces needed food or other attention. They were not pretty children with their thin hair and black eyes too close together. They had their father's face, small and anxious. This face is how Vole got his name. I felt sorry for these girls living with my brother and his wife.

The oldest one came closer to watch me. I wondered when she would have her first blood. Then we would get a new hunter in camp.

"What does the basket say?" the girl asked, for she could see I was listening.

I gave her some stripped branches and showed her how to make the base of a coil. "I will watch for birds at the drying racks," I promised. I told her what my mother had told me. "As you move the willow, think about the river. Think about water. That will make the plant trust you."

My own basket grew perfectly, like a child in the womb. It felt fine to be here alone in such a good place. Once again on the low pink bluff, our tents rose like trees and we had a view of the plains stretching south around a sharp-toothed mountain. Four winters had scoured this old camp clean, and we had not yet littered it with new debris. The youngest child slept. The oldest bent over her work. The willow branches whispered. They had grown so fast, so straight, so strong!

As afternoon passed, the shadows of the drying racks lengthened. Etol and Vole came first, dragging my father, whose bloody face slanted down. Flesh torn from his cheek hung over his chin and part of his nose had been sliced away, leaving a red hole. Blood also soaked through his ripped shirt, so that I knew he had terrible wounds in his chest and shoulder.

I did not look at Etol but screamed for my aunt and ran for my father. As we pulled him into the tent, his eyes rolled back, and he seemed to stop breathing. I screamed again. My aunt was beside me with a bag of moss. Now the tent was full of people. We heard Crane's voice outside, shrill and sharp, like a blue jay in the trees. Vole stared at my father's face and stumbled out the flap of the tent. I also hurried to get a gourd of water.

Near the central fire, I saw Etol sitting on the ground,

holding his knees and weeping. Crane's middle daughter huddled beside him. Then I asked myself, "Where is Dipper? Where are Crow and Second Crow?"

Crane shrieked.

Then I knew everything.

"We did not see the giant short-faced bear and we did not smell her. She came out of the brush so quickly. We did not know that a short-faced bear lived here, near this field, in this part of the forest. She must have left her winter cave early and traveled fast. It has been so dry this spring, so warm, and anyway, there she was, angry for some reason. These bears are like that, I know, but I think this one had some special anger. I think I saw her teats swollen with milk. Maybe she had just lost a cub. We have never seen her tracks in this part of the forest! That is why my wife thought it was safe to get these roots. Etol, Father, and I did not hear or smell anything. We did not see any scat or markings. We were not expecting her. She jumped through the bushes like a lion, just as fast, and she was so big, taller than my tent."

Vole paused. The memory of the bear still frightened him. We call them short-faced bears because their muzzle is blunt like a cat's muzzle, like our own. Their teeth and claws are as long as my hand. They have long legs too, and their feet face forward so that they can stand up like a human being. On the plain, from afar, I have seen a giant short-faced bear stalk and kill a full-grown buffalo.

"None of us heard her," Vole said again. "Dipper, Crow, and Second Crow were digging by the edge of the field, the first ones in her way. They were the closest. I think the little ones died quickly. One after another, with one paw, she smashed their heads. She hit Dipper in the neck. I think Dipper died quickly too. Then she began to eat Dipper. Our father ran forward and threw his spear. He missed! Even though it was so close, he missed! The bear mostly wanted to eat Dipper, but she rose and struck our father across the face and chest. Etol and I also threw our spears and hit her in the arm and shoulder, not enough to kill or bring much blood. Still, she did not like those spears sticking out of her and she tore at them as we grabbed our father and ran backward. My wife and daughter were already running. We all ran. The bear did not chase us. She was busy with Dipper and the spears."

Vole stopped.

He would tell this story only once. He would not want to tell it again, how the bear surprised the hunters, how the woman and children died. We would not want the sorrow of this to settle in the grass, near the baskets or the tents or the fire. A story like that, lifting into the air, might bring the bear herself all the way through the spruce and pine forest, curious to hear how the humans spoke about her, how they praised her good hunt.

For this, I knew, is how the bear thought of my child, little Crow. My child was a good hunt. She was food down the bear's throat, digesting in her stomach, making her feel strong.

I let myself see that. I let myself see Crow torn apart, swallowed, becoming the bear.

I had lost two daughters to this animal. I lost Ali to the shaman spirit of the giant short-faced bear, and I lost Crow to the teeth of the same bear, not a gentle plant-eater like the mammoth but a hunter like us—a better hunter in many ways. This animal could defeat a group of five adults. If the others had not run, they would be dead too.

In the next few days, Etol cried bitterly for his wife and two children. I put my hand on his arm, hiding my impatience. I did not feel his grief. I could barely feel his arm.

At night we lay together in my tent, sharing the warmth of our exhausted bodies. Over and over, I saw Crow's death. I saw the bear tear her small brown face. I was sorry we did not have her bones to bury, bones so tender they had certainly been eaten too. As she became the bear, her time of remembering would come later, when the bear died and moved through soil.

But what would Crow have to remember? She was so young. Her years as a human being were so short. Sometimes I saw the sadness of that, far away like a hill on the horizon. Sometimes I felt a sadness under my feet, deeply buried but still powerful, like a tremor in the earth.

At night I thought of how many animals I had become, animals who became me when I ate them.

Only I rarely ate their bones. That was the difference.

Sometimes, naturally, we crack bones for fat, especially mammoth bones. But usually we let the skeleton lie on the ground to crumble in the dirt or be carried away by scavengers. I tried to remember all those bones. I wondered what had happened to them.

We did not go to a gathering that year. We did not want the sadness of our story traveling with us. Etol and Vole returned to the field in the forest and brought back the skull of my cousin Dipper, who we buried with red ochre and all her tools. They found nothing of Crow or Second Crow.

By then my father was also dead. A younger man might have survived those wounds. Even my father might have lived if he had not been so sorry at the death of his niece, great-nephew and grandchild. Like Vole, the memory of that giant short-faced bear scared him. He never wanted to see that bear again.

My aunt followed in her sleep. I think she must have felt very lonely. Her parents, husband, sister, brother-in-law, and daughter were dead. Her sons had gone to the shaman's camp. For the first time, Sage spoke of two other children, babies who did not live outside my aunt's womb. Her life had been long. We understood why she wanted to rest.

We were more concerned for ourselves, left with only one elder, my sister's husband Bram. I did not even know who had learned my aunt's stories! Who would tell the stories in the winter lodge? Who would be our healer?

Suddenly we were weak. In one spring we had lost three adults and two children. We had lost our confidence and pride. This was a good time, I thought, for me to die as well. My son could take care of himself. My daughters were gone. I did not want to live through the bad changes ahead. Like my aunt, I felt tired.

As he often did, Chi knew what I was thinking. One morning he skinned a rabbit, stewed it with greens, and brought me a bowl.

"Eat this," he said, his voice angry. "Eat more food. You look ugly. I am ashamed to have a mother who looks so ugly."

Soon after, I began to feel the pain. It was like an animal scratching in my chest, scratching and biting. I missed Crow every day and Second Crow too. Sometimes I expected my little daughter to run into our tent with her black hair flapping. I felt an emptiness in camp, places where she should have been, holes in the air.

I also missed my father and aunt. This sadness was less because they were old and happier now, moving through soil.

Strangely, I missed Dipper the most. We had grown up together. All my life I had heard her voice, seen her face, smelled her body. I had been at the birth of her oldest and youngest child. Often I scorned her. I thought her silly and vain. When we were children, we made little tents out of animal scraps and I hurried home with pieces of meat for her to cook.

Late one night, under the bearskin, I felt its triumph. My cousin killed your cousin, the skin whispered.

Etol and Chi still slept. Breathing hard, I ran to the central fire and fed it more wood. Then I took that skin and burnt it until the smoke and smell made my relatives wake and come out of their tents. Chi was horrified. His father's bearskin! Sparks flew up orange and yellow. The stars glittered. I realized too late that I done this skin a favor. Now the bear was free.

Part Two

Chapter Six

Mammoths too are interested in bones. When Red Fur and her family see the remains of a mammoth, they stop to smell the carcass, picking up a piece, putting it down, picking up another. Their trunks curl around a dried shin or rib cage. They caress and fondle certain bones, especially the tusks and dirty-white skull. If they recognize this as a family member, they will stay a long time, even when there is no grass. Sometimes they scatter bones, each mammoth taking one to carry. I do not know if they do this for friends or for enemies. I have also seen them bury mammoths. In my dream of the future, after the female bled to death, the matriarch covered the body with branches, bushes, and dirt until it was a mound, something built on the plain, in the way we build tents and lodges. Tenderly Red Fur also buried the baby. Like us, they do not care about the bones of other animals but leave these to lie unattended.

I know these things because in the years after Crow was eaten I saw many, many mammoth bones. I watched Half Ear and her family move up and down the dying river, trampling all the narrow-leafed trees, and I saw other herds too as they traveled through the forests of juniper and pine, looking for water. Now when the groups met, they spread their ears and jerked their heads rapidly. Sometimes the matriarch and Red Fur chased the strangers away. Once I saw Half Ear drive her tusk deep into the leg of a female. Usually these new groups were small, members of a herd that had broken apart.

The mammoths suffered because the eye of Old Man watched us too closely, too often, with great interest. One spring when we moved from the winter lodge, we saw that the water by our summer camp on the bluff had stopped flowing. Every day the remaining pools grew smaller. As the river dried up, the mammoths looked for springs and ponds, and so did we. In the sandy streambeds, they used their tusks to scoop up the earth and dig wells. We did the same. It was not hard for us to get enough water for our needs. But mammoths must drink great amounts, especially in the summer. Their wells were not big enough for everyone in their group.

In the years after Crow died, the mammoths also began to die, some of them all at once. This was a wonderful time for me and my family. Daily I walked the plain with Wolf, Chi, Etol, and his sons. Whenever we saw signs of a herd, we followed them, hoping to find a big pile of bodies. If the mammoths were too badly rotted, we only took ivory. Most times we ate the meat too, fresh or spoiled, and filled our packs to carry home. Sometimes we had to kill dying animals or healthy ones who had not yet abandoned their relatives. In this way, I became a mammoth hunter again. But it was not the same kind of hunting. These mammoths died too easily. Out of grief or sickness, they waited for the spear. We killed them on the plain, and we killed them in the forest, and we killed them near the ponds where the water turned to mud and then to dust.

Other predators and scavengers enjoyed this feast. Teratorns and vultures often led us to our prey. Afterward they made us curse and lose our tempers. When these birds spread their wings, they were as tall as Etol. When we threatened them, they moved back a step—only to crowd in again, great groups of many types and sizes. We also had to compete with dire wolves, gray wolves, lions, coyotes, wildcats, and wild dogs. Sometimes, with two or more mammoths dead on the ground, I found myself butchering one body while a pair of wolves tore at another. I was so close I could hear them chew and see their teeth dripping blood and flesh. With plenty for all, we worried less about being eaten ourselves. In a big die-off, we might all work near each other, humans, wolves, dogs, and cats, while the birds plunged in their beaks.

We gathered so much ivory we hardly had time to carve it. In the winter, everyone now had a necklace to make or beads to sew on shirts and pants.

In other ways we were also lucky. The family whose son had joined ours kept their promise. Their second son married Crane's oldest daughter, a woman at last, ugly and shy.

Next when we went to the spring gathering, two sisters approached us, the first and second wife of a husband who beat them. In their arms, each carried a baby girl. They wanted to leave that man before they had sons who must grow up with the father. They wanted to leave relatives who had mistreated them after their parents' death.

Now Wolf could have a wife in his own camp!

This good news caused problems we could not easily solve. The women's family were furious, although we offered them a big supply of ivory. But this family had collected ivory of their own. Mammoths were dying everywhere. Suddenly many of us were wealthy, and ivory lost its power. We all became confused about the nature of marriage gifts. Still these women wanted to go with us, and their relatives had to agree. When the husband threatened Etol, the women's own brother held the man back. We knew we would always have trouble with this group.

Early in these talks, I pushed forward and asked that the second sister be given to Chi.

Etol hesitated. "I also have two boys, the children of Dipper, who need wives," he said.

I had thought that far. "These baby girls can grow up to be their wives. They are not from our lineage."

"It is a long time to wait," Crane interfered.

"Chi is older," I insisted. "He needs a wife now."

"Not much older," Crane said. "And does this woman want him? We cannot force her. We do not want these women to go elsewhere."

Crane looked smug. Her black eyebrows rose.

But she was right. The second sister did not want to marry a younger man. In that matter, however, the women of our camp were firm. None of *our* husbands needed a second wife. We could only offer her a choice of the three boys.

This woman said she would come with us and decide later. Unfortunately that summer her teeth began to hurt. Two of them became infected and the woman went crazy with pain. Her moans filled our camp and made us cry too. At last, to everyone's relief, she died. Wolf and his new wife took in the baby girl.

After that, there were no more deaths but many births. Dipper's daughter had a boy. Crane's daughter became pregnant quickly and also had a boy. When Wolf's stepdaughters were past weaning, his wife had twins, two more girls! By then both Dipper and Crane's daughter each had a girl too. Finally Crane herself had a boy. Our camp was full of children, meat, and ivory. From weakness and despair, we were strong again. Our good fortune amazed us.

Crane, who was my age, nursed a child. But I had no more babies myself. Two times my stomach swelled and each time a bloody mass came out too soon. I buried the remains without red ochre, for they were not yet human. Etol said he was content. We hunted together and he liked mating whenever he wanted. Now he had grandchildren from Dipper's daughter to carry around camp. Cheerfully he made them toys and played the games that babies love. Their black hair flapped like a crow's wings. I was careful never to say this out loud.

For a long time it seemed I could not hold a baby. Then

my brother's wife had twins and I helped care for the smallest, tucking the little girl under my breast. She could not suckle but she liked the warmth. She felt safe.

By this time, Chi was older than Jak had been when I married him. I remember the day Chi killed the matriarch Half Ear.

A group of us—Etol, his sons, Wolf, Chi, and myself—had walked a long way from our summer camp, looking for places to quarry stone. Where the plain moved up into a small hill, above a cluster of oak trees, we lay on our stomachs and watched the mammoth herd grazing below. The summer grass was dry and yellow. Each mammoth had to twirl her trunk around a clump of stems, kick at its base, and pull sharply. Then the animal beat the clump against her knees to knock off the dust and chaff. As she chewed at the remains, she twirled her trunk around a new clump, kicked, and pulled. Except for the youngest calves, all the mammoths concentrated on this task. Where the grass grew greener, smaller animals gave way to larger ones, their feet swinging in the submissive posture.

The matriarch stood alone. Like Red Fur, one of her tusks had broken off. The other looked dirty, pocked, and gouged. She did not eat but hung her head, her trunk on the ground, her shoulders slumping.

"She is sick," Etol guessed.

"She is old," I said. By now I had butchered many old mammoths and I knew that Half Ear's teeth were worn to stubs. She could no longer chew bark and branches. Even this coarse yellow grass required too much effort.

Etol agreed. "Your father knew her when he hunted mammoths. You are right. She is old. She is dying."

"I want her tusk," Chi said.

I did not turn to see Etol stare at Chi, but I felt my husband's dismay. Once the tusks of the matriarch would have been a prize, well worth waiting for. Now we had more than enough ivory, and this tusk was broken and stained. On this trip we had not planned to hunt mammoths. We carried empty packs in the hope of finding flint, quartz, and chert. For a share of what we brought back, Bram would make us each a fluted point, perfectly shaped for our bones in the grave.

Lying in the grass behind Chi, I watched my son rise to get a better look at the mammoth herd. Their poor vision could not see this far, and the wind blew our way, the scent of mammoths mingling with chalky soil. In the clear morning light, I admired my son's body. His chest and stomach were outlined in muscle. His brown skin gleamed like a piece of chert moistened to bring out the red. His black braided hair was long and thick, another sign of good health.

A handsome man, I thought, despite the yellow scars that pucker his shoulder. Our young people give us this kind of pleasure. They decorate our camp.

Etol watched me watch Chi. If my son insisted on staying by the mammoth herd, I would stay with him. Then Etol and Wolf would have to decide whether to help kill the matriarch or leave us to fill their packs with stone. Etol's sons would go where their father went. I envied him that. Chi had never been so easy.

If Vole had been here, he would have been blunt. "It is not a victory to kill an old mammoth," he would have said to my son. "Are you a hunter or a collector of ivory? You have more ivory than anyone in this family."

These were the insults Chi lived with. Privately the other men mocked his love of tusks, the way he took ivory whenever he could, however he could. They said Chi was not a hunter like Jak but a scavenger, a teratorn, intent on the scenes of death.

Chi watched the mammoth herd. Etol and Wolf watched him. Wiser than Vole, they said nothing. Chi was a grown man quick to anger. He was strong and could carry big loads on his back. If he wanted to stay and kill the matriarch, Etol and Wolf would not stop him.

Suddenly the huge animal collapsed to her knees. Red Fur bellowed and rushed to stand beside her mother. But the daughter did not try and hold up the matriarch with her remaining tusk. Slowly, crumbling, Half Ear rolled over on her side. All the older females gathered around, trumpeting, screaming, flapping their ears. Only the young males and calves kept grazing, too hungry to stop, moving eagerly into the green grass left by the adults.

"This will not take long," Chi whispered.

"That's hard to know," Etol disagreed. "Those of us who need stone should go ahead. We can meet you here later."

"If the mammoth travels, I will follow her," Chi warned.

"Then we will meet you at camp," Etol replied. "We will have flint to carry. The ivory is yours."

I was not pleased to be one of two hunters alone on the plain. Also, I had wanted stone too. That evening, my irritation showed in the clumsy way I built a fire. Chi hardly noticed. In this matter, he was still like a child, used to people moving sadly or happily around him, interested only in his own feelings.

It is hard to stay angry at night when the glowing face of Old Woman bends close to the earth. The stars press down strongly on us human beings, squeezing out our thoughts and stories because their stories are so much bigger. Flashes of light show where a hunter in the sky has made a kill, and I have seen nights when the hunters went wild and lights flashed brightly everywhere. In the middle of Old Woman's forehead flows a white river where animals drink and clouds of gnats hover and whine. Some of us believe that when our bones turn to dust and nothing remains in the ground to remember, we will rise to live with the stars in the sky. Like my bearskin, we will dance and drink from the white river.

On the flank of a hill, I trampled down the brittle yellow grass and built a fire of scrub-oak branches. Then I prepared to take my turn awake against lions and wolves. Before he slept, Chi asked me to tell him about White Bear and Dog. In the starry darkness lit by a flickering light, I could almost believe that he was a boy again, that Ali and Crow were safe nearby. My breast hurt with these old pains. Even so, I was glad now to be alone with my son, talking him into sleep.

"This is a story from the north and our journey here to this land." I pointed up, directly above me. "There is White Bear, who never leaves the sky but circles endlessly that bright star. Holding on to White Bear's tail is an animal called Wolverine, a creature also from the north, small and fierce. White Bear and Wolverine did not want human beings to come into this country. They guarded a mountain pass that on each side had great boulders of ice and rock. The only way to the valley below, full of green plants, was through the mountain pass surrounded by ice. White Bear and Wolverine let all the animals enter the valley. They let the mammoth walk through, shaking the ground with her big feet, and the mastodon and the camel and the buffalo and the deer and the musk ox and the tapir and the saber-toothed cat and the lion and the short-faced bear and the cheetah and the gray wolf and the red wolf and all the little animals like squirrels and voles. But they would not let human beings come safely between the giant rocks through the ice.

"Now, human beings had one good friend among the animals and that was Dog. You can see Dog with his long tail. He also lives in the north and never leaves the sky. Dog went to White Bear and whispered, 'Every day the human beings come to this mountain pass and every day you drive them away. I have a trick that will help you get rid of the human beings forever.'

"White Bear was suspicious. He knew that Dog was

friendly with humans and even lived with them in their camps. But Dog said with a show of innocence, 'Do I not have fur like you? Do I not run on four feet like you? Why would I protect the human beings instead of my own kind?'

"So White Bear went to Wolverine. . . ."

93

This is a long story with many surprises and funny scenes where Dog fools White Bear and upsets Wolverine. Chi laughed in all the right places as he stared into the sky where Bear and Dog chase each other.

At the end, he thanked me and asked, "Why do we not have camp dogs?"

I shrugged. "Your uncle did not like dogs. He said they were too much trouble."

"Huh," Chi said, thinking it over. "Our uncle has been in the ground a long time."

I added new branches to the fire.

When enough had burned, I woke Chi and went to sleep.

By morning, Half Ear lay so still we thought she was dead. Even so, her family had not left her. Now I could recognize only a few members of this herd. Red Fur stood out strong and capable, despite her broken tusk. Little Ivory had died a few summers ago but Big Ivory remained with a thin calf sucking her teat. Little Penis and Big Penis were gone. Other adolescent males took their place. All together, the group was half its former size. They had done better than most in this long drought because they knew the land so well and because the matriarch was a good leader. When the grass died, she made the herd browse on scrub brush and took them deep into the spruce forests to strip bark from long-needled trees. When the water holes dried, she showed them where to dig wells. If she smelled smoke from a fire, she pushed and prodded the herd to run.

"How long will they stay with her?" Chi asked.

"With good grass, they would stay a long time. Now I do not know. The calves are so thin. They have to move."

"Who is the new matriarch?"

"We call her Red Fur."

"Would a spear in her rump hurry her along?"

"You're too impatient," I told my son. "A lot of mammoths are here, and they are nervous and unhappy. The old matriarch is dying. We only have to wait."

Red Fur did not make us wait long. Late that morning she sent out a rumble, turned, and began to walk south. The others followed slowly for the calves were weak. A few of the mammoths kept stopping to look behind, but Red Fur went on without a pause.

As soon as they were out of sight, we went down the little hill and approached Half Ear lying on the ground. Buffalo birds, perched on her stomach, rose in the air. Engorged with blood, fat ticks as big as my fist covered her fur. Long thin worms crawled from her anus, and flies hovered around her crusted eyes. We saw that her sides heaved with ragged breathing. The matriarch was still alive! Sick, unconscious, swarming with pests, she still looked powerful. She still carried power in the round hump of her shoulder and in the dark trunk and stained ivory.

Her eyelids moved. I wondered if she knew we were there. Did she feel frightened? Or was she dreaming, falling into death through memories of grass and water holes where calves wriggled in black mud and climbed on each other's backs, squealing and trumpeting? The herds met and en- 95
twined their trunks, gently knocking tusks. She dreamed of being a young female, when the bulls chased her and she slowed to let herself be caught, when her babies were born and she felt that delicious pull at her teat, when her own mother died, the sorrow of that, the sorrow when she became the matriarch.

Chi used the atlatl. My husband had been wrong. Chi had not started too late. My son stepped back, aimed the throwing stick, and threw his spear into Half Ear's neck. The mammoth shuddered as her blood gushed out and pooled on the ground. She bled to death quickly. I watched Chi's face. When he did not smile, I felt glad.

I let him do the work of cutting out the tusk.

"Do you remember when she killed my father?" he asked.

This surprised me. I had forgotten about that.

"Of course," I said. "It was a long time ago."

"This ivory is for you," Chi told me. "I will carve you a necklace from the matriarch's tusk."

Again I was surprised. "Thank you," I said.

Chapter Seven

Unlike mammoths, we do not choose a matriarch but have different leaders, male and female. My sister was one of these. Sage had listened carefully to our aunt's stories and could repeat them all, with the same words and the same lilt in her voice, rising for drama, lowering for importance. In the winter lodge, Sage remembered our long journey here, telling it again as we sat by the fire or lay under our skins. I was someone who knew about White Bear and Dog, funny tales meant to entertain. But Sage knew our history, the way our family stretched back daughter to daughter, son to son.

Sage said that Tewa, the first woman to enter this country, was the mother of our grandmother's grandmother. We do not really know how many generations have passed since Tewa's journey. But we do believe that our family group comes directly from Tewa and her husband, Tono, that we are their children.

Our ancestors lived in a strange place. Sometimes the sun shone in the night as well as in the day, and sometimes the night lasted all day long. It must have been confusing as Old Man and Old Woman fought and bickered, one gaining control of the sky and then the other. Their struggles could be seen in lights and colors that flared on the horizon, bursts of anger and joy. In this cold violent land, great winds bent the fir trees. Storms of ice killed anyone who could not find shelter. Winter lasted three times as long, and the people had to live in lodges most of the year, thigh to thigh, sharing the same fire.

Fortunately they were used to this closeness. Before coming here, their own grandmothers had been in another country crowded with human beings. There the hunting grounds were small and groups fought as they met too often, killing each other over a cliff of chert or a dead mammoth.

So those grandmothers had traveled to this land of ice where Tewa and Tono married young and struggled to raise their children. Unlike Old Man and Old Woman, they never argued. They were strong because they acted as one instead of two. Tewa had five boys and five girls. Each child lived to be an adult and to have more children. Her husband, Tono, was an exceptional hunter who had never been injured. Both Tewa and Tono were clever, healthy, and brave.

One day they took their large family and walked south to find another, better place to live.

When Sage told this story, her voice deepened on the word *south* and I thought of Ali, whose voice had done the same thing when she said she was going south with the shaman. Perhaps Ali had learned that deepness from my old aunt. When my daughter thought of walking south, perhaps she thought of Tewa and Tono, who had never argued but mated happily every single night.

This was a hard journey, Sage told us. There were many days when the way ahead of Tono's family looked worse than the way behind. Snowstorms raged and mountains blocked the path. But Tewa and Tono were determined. They knew about the land they had left behind. They wanted to see what was ahead. Only strong leadership could have brought so many people so far and so fast. Only a family tied with trust and blood could have survived. If the women complained or scolded, they would have taken away the men's strength. If the men were foolish or arrogant, they would not have listened to the women. They would not know which plants to eat or which way to go.

When Sage came to this part of the story, her voice also lowered—because this was important. We had heard it many times before. Still we murmured our agreement. Living cramped and bored in the winter lodge, we had to be careful. We had to keep our family tied with trust and blood. If we had been lazy that day, if we whined about the food, we shifted uncomfortably under our skins. We promised ourselves we would try harder.

At least, this was Sage's intent when she lowered her voice.

Tewa and Tono were old the day they started their journey. They got older as the group stopped to rest and have babies. They wondered why they did not see any signs of other human beings, any footprints, lodges, snares, or fires. When a hunter approached a mammoth or antelope, the creature watched until a stone pierced his heart. Then he fell down in amazement. Other members of the herd saw the collapse and came over curiously. They looked around in alarm. Where was the danger? They had never been bitten from such a distance. They had never known a claw that could come in the wind.

Slowly Tewa and Tono realized that this land had no people of its own. This land was new. It even had animals that Tewa's family had not seen before, newly made animals, awkward and clumsy. In this land, Old Man and Old Woman were at peace and ruled the sky each in turn, round and hot, round and cold.

One night Tewa had a dream in which she saw the children of her children's children. They had spread across this land and their lodges were full of meat, ivory, and babies. Tewa's dream had slipped into the future. When she cried out with happiness, her husband woke and mated with her. The next day, they celebrated with a dance for the camels.

At this point, Sage always stopped and looked around. Sometimes she spread her arms as if to enclose us. Surely our lodge was the one Tewa had seen in her dream. Surely we sat here surrounded by meat, ivory, and babies who crawled over the adults trying to listen. We were Tewa's dream. We were the future.

We all felt the wonder of that.

The story of our journey could take most of the night. The next morning we would sleep late and hunt in the afternoon. Sage did a good job, much better than our old aunt, who had sometimes grown distracted or tired. In the winter lodge, when my sister's hands moved in the firelight, I felt proud of her. None of us had guessed she had such talent. Her husband, Bram, was also proud. Her status now added to his.

In the day, of course, Sage was just Sage. We often worked together scraping furs and making clothes. One afternoon in the winter's lodge, Crane's oldest daughter entered through the flap on her hands and knees, her little girl on her hip. The baby's fat legs clamped tightly around the mother's pants and the child's eyes gleamed black in the round face. Crane's daughter rarely put this bird down. Her husband and son followed, the boy after his father, imitating the man's gestures. They were excited, and we were happy to see them. This was a family whose pleasure in each other made us feel good.

"Look what we have." My niece spoke to me.

"A squirrel!" the boy put in, eager to tell the news.

Crane's daughter showed us a gathering basket full of pine nuts. Her husband carried a second basket. They had found the cache of a hardworking squirrel. In their arms, they had all his winter storage. The boy was gleeful.

"We have brought them for everyone," he exclaimed.

"You are generous," Sage smiled at him. "We will shell them for you and roast them tonight."

"I hope you have not eaten any," I teased the child. "I hope you brought them all back to share."

I did not see Crane entering the lodge too.

I was only teasing the boy. Naturally Crane's daughter had let her children fill their stomachs with pine nuts. By sharing what remained, she earned for her family a part of

what someone else might share. In the winter, we eat whenever we can. Above all, we love nuts and seeds and anything
green. Hunters even take the green food from the stomachs
of the deer they kill. For shelling these pine nuts, I would
also take a few handfuls, eating as I shelled.

But Crane spoke to me in a shocked voice as though I
had insulted her grandson.

Sage answered her quickly, explaining that I meant no
harm.

Crane's daughter hurried to say that we were joking and
that I had offered to shell the nuts for tonight. At this, Crane
only looked more irritated.

I was irritated too. I could speak for myself.

Wrinkling her nose, Crane went to her living area, grabbed
some furs, and left. Her daughter's family followed, less happy
than before.

Sage shook her head and took one of the baskets. I took
the other and ate the first nut I opened. The tiny sliver, as
small as a fingernail, tasted deliciously sweet.

Without speaking, my sister and I agreed not to discuss
our older brother's wife. For one thing, she might return at
any moment. For another, she was Sage's stepdaughter, and
we wanted to avoid an argument. Sage expected me to be
more patient with Crane, even more friendly. I thought I
was as patient and as friendly as possible. Crane was like an
injury that would not heal. This winter she had been more
difficult than usual.

"This winter is long," my sister said.

"I am thinking of spring," I answered as I cracked my nuts, the shells in one pile, the meat in another. "Our niece's husband tells me there is a girl in his family near her monthly blood. Her grandmother's grandmother was our mother's aunt."

"Then she is of our lineage."

"No," I said. "Our mother never really knew this aunt, who traveled north before she came to live with our niece's husband's group. There have been many children since then."

"The aunt of our mother is our lineage," Sage said flatly. "If she comes from this aunt, she is too."

It seemed we were going to argue after all.

"Other men and women like this have married," I protested. "You keep track of lineage too closely."

"You want this girl for Chi." Sage never stopped her work. Only once in a while, her hand traveled to her mouth and she spoke through the chewed pine nuts. "Do you think these parents would want this too?"

I nodded slowly, pretending I had not thought about the problem before. "It would require gifts—and better ones than ivory. Still, that family is tied to us. Their sons are here. We could visit often."

Sage did not answer. It was a strong discouragement. I had not really hoped too much for this match. Others would also argue about lineage.

"You want Chi to marry," my sister said suddenly. "But is that the best thing?"

I grunted in surprise.

"Chi does not want to leave this camp," Sage continued. "He has said so himself."

"Chi needs a wife. He needs children."

My sister's expression did not change.

"Have you spoken with him?" she asked only.

An old jealousy pinched my ear. Chi and Sage had talked about this. My son had gone to his aunt for advice. I answered sharply, cracking my nuts, making two piles. "There's nothing to say. You may be right. That girl may not make a good marriage. If there's a large gathering this spring, there will be other girls."

"Do you remember how Mother used to braid our hair?" Sage could do this, turn her thoughts in any direction. "She used a red dye on strips of leather."

"The bark of the alder." I remembered too.

"We should make those strips for Wolf's children. I haven't seen that red for a long time."

"It is harder to find alder now," I reminded Sage. "That tree loves water."

Sage nodded in a way that made me feel wise. This was one of her gifts.

When I was young, I often followed my older sister and watched her braid move back and forth, the red leather mixed with black. Sometimes we gathered the bark of alder in winter, which was a good time to eat other kinds of bark from the juniper tree or shaman's bush. In the spring, Mother found stinging nettle and boiled the roots to make a yellow dye. Another root from bird grass gave the color purple. Our longest days of gathering were in the summer, when we only had to stretch out our hands to find them brimming over with seeds. Nearly every day we had a bowl of mush and one of green leaves boiled with herbs. Tasting my saliva, I ate another handful of pine nuts.

Pine trees can be old and calm. Pine trees are generous. Their brown nuts pop quickly out of the cone and the coat of the seed is easy to break. The rich oily smell is comforting. Eating these nuts, I saw that busy squirrel squeaking in delight and stuffing his cheeks until they bulged.

Like Sage, I thought of my mother.

She was a woman who loved feathers—blue feathers from jays, red feathers from cardinals, shimmering feathers from waterbirds. Whenever one of my brothers killed a turkey, he brought her the body and she went through the tail, picking out the plumage to sew on the skirt she wore when dancing. Once at a gathering, my father made a trade for the dried body of a parrot from the south. These feathers were red, orange, and green. Smiling, Mother sewed them onto the skirt in which she was buried. I was glad to think of that parrot talking to her now.

Our mother was never as clever as our aunt. Small and not strong, she was famous only for making a girl's tattoo at her first blood. On Sage's thigh she used an obsidian flake to prick the pattern of a cat's claw, a powerful mark for a young girl. Later she rubbed brown liquid into the wound so the color would stay under the scar. My mother died before I had my own tattoo. Now I could no longer see her face. I remembered her hands better, short fingered and stained with the red of alder.

"Do you remember when Mother marked you?" I asked Sage. "You and Dipper together. We ate a lot that day. It was a good spring for ground berries."

"This will be a good spring for roots," Sage predicted.

We were comfortable now talking about food, as people often do at the end of winter.

Once again I put aside Chi's marriage.

The cold wind annoyed us when Crane's daughter pushed the flap and let her baby crawl forward, the little mouth open, the black eyes spilling tears. Crane's daughter followed and picked up the child. She also looked as though she wanted to cry.

"Mother wants us to build a tent." Crane's daughter spoke directly to Sage. "She wants her children and husband and my children and husband and her father and you to live outside in a tent while the rest of the group stay in the lodge. She says the lodge is too crowded."

Sage rose. "What is Crane doing now?"

"My mother is upset," Crane's daughter said. "She has covered herself with furs and sits under a tree. She says she will not move."

Chapter Eight

If Sage had not looked so serious, I would have laughed at the sight of Crane huddled in her furs under a scrubby plum thicket. Piled around her shoulders and feet were the skins of many different animals, bear and bobcat, fox and rabbit, so that she looked like a strange animal herself, a mixed-up creature. I snorted and covered my mouth, but no one else shared my amusement. Etol crouched anxiously beside his sister. Vole stood with his arms crossed like two ropes binding his chest. Crane's daughter held her little girl while her husband took the hand of his son. Crane seemed to be the center of everyone's attention. This, of course, was exactly what she wanted.

Sage spoke reasonably. "Crane, stepdaughter, a tent and a lodge need twice as much wood, twice as much work to keep a fire burning. Your family will not be as warm in this tent. And we will miss you in the lodge."

"My family wants to live in its own tent." Crane's voice shook, uncertain. "You and my father must live with us. That lodge is too crowded. We are stepping on each other's toes."

"Winter is nearly over," Sage tried again. "This is a bad example for our children. Soon we will be moving to a summer camp. Let us stay in the lodge a little longer."

Etol glanced at me but I had nothing to say.

"It is a lot of work building a winter tent," Etol warned Crane as he put a hand on her shoulder. "Does your family want to do this work?"

Vole said quickly, "I will do the work. I will do the work! But my sister Sage may be right. Winter is almost over. Maybe we can wait a little longer."

Even Crane's daughter spoke now, and this was bold for her. "We will be more crowded in a tent than in the lodge," the girl whispered.

Furiously Crane began to kick at the furs on the ground. She stood up, her arms whirling, her leather shoes stamping up and down. I was astonished. This woman acted like a child who had not been weaned. If my own child had such a tantrum, I would walk away with a show of distaste. Yet here we were, crowded around my sister-in-law, talking and pleading.

I tried to get Etol's attention. Let's go, I gestured with my hands. No. He shook his head. Etol! I widened my eyes. He looked ashamed. He could not leave his sister. Wah! I wrinkled my nose.

Crane wept, mucus and tears sliding down her face. Her voice rose to its normal pitch, shrill and unpleasant. Yes, she shouted at her daughter, a tent would be too crowded! She did not really want to live in a tent! She wanted to live in the lodge! But it was so unpleasant there! She and her family were treated without respect! She was the daughter of the oldest man in camp and the wife of the second oldest! It would be more fair if she and her family stayed in the lodge and Etol and his family built themselves a tent outside! That would be more fair! That was what she really wanted. Then she would be happy. Then she would know people appreciated her.

My amazement filled the earth and sky. If my aunt were alive, she would slap this woman twice across both cheeks. Sage needed to act quickly.

Moving closer to my sister, I encouraged her. "She is your stepdaughter. Teach her some manners."

Vole overheard. "Do not speak about my wife!" he yelled. "This is your fault! You are the cause of this!"

"What?" I screamed.

Insanely I wished I had my spear.

My brother moved toward me, his fists clenched.

Etol stepped between us.

Sage clapped three times, so hard it must have hurt.

"We will leave!" Crane shrilled. "We will leave this camp!"

Now everyone was silent as we turned to stare at her. Crane also looked stunned. One hand crept up to cover her mouth, and we kept staring, our eyes on that hand, waiting for her to take the words back.

"Yes," she went on after a long moment. "We will leave this camp since we are treated so rudely. My husband, children and grandchildren, my father, my stepmother . . ."

"Do not speak for me." Sage's voice was cold.

"No," Crane faltered, and said nothing more.

Vole's fists loosened against his leather pants. He looked at his wife and daughter, at his open palms. His small eyes darted and his body seemed to jerk, snared in pride. Vole is stubborn. In his mind, he had allied with Crane, allowing her to go this far. He had lost control of his wife and he could not admit that. For different reasons, he was as helpless as Etol.

Sage stood stiff with anger. Her arms hugged her breasts. "We will talk about this tonight around the fire," she said. "Everyone must go and think about this. Think about what this will mean to our children and their children, for sisters and brothers to part over an argument, for even husbands and wives to part."

With these last words, she looked at Bram.

"Think about this," Sage said, "each one of you."

Winter snows can make us drowsy, happy to be inside our lodge, the world outside white and clean. The drifts of snow turn this land into a new story and even the black branches of trees look unfamiliar. The bushes are strange, humped shapes. The sky is bluer next to the white. Later, when our icy pants melt by the fire and the lodge gets muddy, we grow irritable. We complain about our wet clothes. Still, the whiteness remains when we shut our eyes. We feel clean and new. This is something that only happens with the snows of winter.

That winter seemed to have few snowstorms. The days were cold and harsh, unbalanced by beauty. The wind dried out the land, dried out our skin until our chapped lips bled and split open. The little snow that fell melted quickly, and the world was brown, gray, and bleak.

Across the fire in our lodge I looked at Crane, at her wide cheekbones, thick eyebrows, flat nose, and strong teeth. When she and Vole met, my brother was overwhelmed by this face. His mouth fell open and he gasped like a fish. I made fun of him then. Many years later, Crane looked less pretty, the mother of three daughters and a son. Still she held on to the power of a woman who could excite men. Across the fire in our lodge, I saw that she would do this. She would divide us. She would hurt her family for the need that rose up in her, the need of the moment. She was nervous. But she was willing.

Breaking up in winter is not uncommon. Crane had seen something like this before, I realized, when she and her father and brothers had left their family group to join ours. Now these children around the fire would always remember how we had broken apart too. Each part would be weaker. Crane did most of our healing and we would lose her skills. Her family would lose their storyteller. These children would learn about weakness, not strength. They would never understand the journey of Tewa and Tono, and we would no longer be part of Tewa's dream. I wondered if this was what bothered Sage the most. I did not know. I had watched her speak earnestly with Vole and with Etol, but for some reason she never approached me.

This is Crane's decision, I thought. Briefly I glanced at Wolf's wife, holding one of her three-year-old twins. She had left her first husband and that had been good for her and good for us. As the second twin joined her, the mother looked distracted. The girls could hardly fit in the space between her breasts and crossed legs. Squirming, the children kicked at each other. Whatever happened tonight, Wolf's wife was not concerned. Wolf and his four daughters would stay with

Sage and me and Etol and his children. It was Vole and Crane who would have the smaller group, who would have to travel to the edge of our hunting grounds, who would have to build a new winter lodge.

I hope it will be comfortable, I thought silently to Crane. I hope no one steps on your toes.

Looking around the fire, I passed quickly over Crane's daughter, her worried face uglier than usual. I saw that the husband of this daughter sat apart with his brother and with Etol's sons. This man did not want to move away with his mother-in-law! Crane's other children also waited uneasily, a grown girl on each side, the little boy in her lap. Vole glared straight ahead. Bram and Etol watched the cooking fire as though they had never seen one before. Sage also stared into the flames. She could not force her stepdaughter.

Our talk began with a polite murmur. Crane said that she and her family had been thinking about this for a long time. They did not want to leave with bad feelings. They hoped that Sage would come with them.

"I will stay here," Sage said quietly.

Crane already knew that. "And my father?" she asked in a hopeful voice.

Bram lifted his hands. "I will stay with my wife and son Etol."

Crane's little boy began to cry, softly at first, because he did not know what was wrong. As he gasped and hiccuped, his mother rocked him with a rough motion, jiggling his bottom. But he would not be comforted. His cries were so gentle our voices could carry over the sound. We talked more loudly. When did Vole's family want to leave and what would they take with them?

I wanted to hold the baby myself. I had never let Chi or Ali cry like that.

In my thoughts, I saw Crane's daughter on the plain, following her willful mother and father, weeping as she carried a heavy pack. Her little boy and girl were also crying because they were tired and hungry and afraid of being so far from the lodge. The child who had shown me his pine nuts suddenly fell, cutting his knees. Now his sobs attracted the attention of two lionesses. The cats began to follow the family, hoping the little boy would lag behind. Crane turned to yell at her grandson. It was all his fault! The husband of Crane's daughter bent his head. In the winter afternoon he wore only his leather pants and shirt, decorated with designs he had brought from his family group. Not once did he look at his wife and children. I wondered how long he would stay with these people.

I thought about how nice our camp would be, without Crane, without Vole. Crane had wanted to tie my daughter with yucca rope. Vole had wanted to hurt me with his fists. I would be happier, more relaxed, without them.

I saw the lionesses creep through the scrub brush. They were so close they could smell the blood from the boy's knees. The wind blew their way. They could smell the humans but the humans could not smell them.

Shaking my head, I rose and went to my living place. I

knew that everyone watched with alarm as I moved aside tools and pushed away furs. From a deerskin bundle, I brought out the necklace that Chi had carved for me from the matriarch's tusk. You have seen this necklace, and you know how heavy it is, how long and impressive. Chi spent a winter making the beads, the sides slightly flattened with a hole drilled carefully through each center. The ivory is not white or flawless. Its cracks make a pattern like a spray of curled ferns. Newly made, Chi's necklace already seemed old.

I gave this necklace to Crane.

"This is more valuable than anything I own," I said to her. Sparks flew from the fire up the smoke hole. I could feel Chi's eyes on my face, on Crane's hand as it dipped under the weight of the ivory beads. "You can take this with you if you want. But I would prefer that you stay here. My husband and I will build a tent outside the lodge and live there with our children and their children for the rest of the winter. I think this is a good idea. I also think the lodge is too crowded. I have become very annoyed with the smoke in here."

Crane's mouth opened but she did not make a sound. Shocked, suspicious, she stared at the necklace looped in her fingers. Her son stopped crying and took a fistful of beads into his mouth. My speech was not as nice as it seemed. The last of it carried a second meaning that Crane understood very well. This was not a real peace between us. Only the necklace was real, heavy and long, thick with beads carved through one winter. The necklace was a substantial gift, an extravagant gift. It could not be ignored.

Vole acted quickly, as quick as a real vole. "That has been our problem! The lodge is too crowded this winter. Now my sister and brother-in-law have offered to move outside. My family is pleased. We will stay here. This has been a bad winter. We should forget this unusual winter. Thank you for the necklace, Willow. It is a sign of your respect."

As fast as that, Crane's plans fell apart. Her husband did not even glance in her direction. Happily her son teethed on my ivory necklace, his tears forgotten as though he had never cried in his life.

We would not be so fortunate. We would spend years recovering from this event.

Crane was smarter than I thought. She kept a close watch on all our exchanges, and this one was unbalanced. "Yes, we will stay," she muttered to herself. "But I cannot take this."

As she thrust the necklace into my hands, her little boy puckered his face. Pulling away the beads had bruised his gums. "I will take another gift as a sign of your respect," Crane went on hurriedly while the baby took a breath, preparing to scream. "The parka lined with wolf fur. That will fit me, I think. This other is too much. Too big."

The child inhaled and shrieked. I moved back from the noise, holding my rejected gift. Truthfully I wanted my wolf parka more than I wanted the matriarch's necklace. Something about these beads bothered me. Something woke me in the night when I sensed their presence, cracked and stained.

Puzzled, I looked back over the day. I had lost my best parka, my family had to build a tent outside, and my son,

Chi, was wrinkling his nose. From all this, I realized that Crane was a very strong woman. When we became enemies, Jak had also been this ruthless.

My sister bent to hide her expression. I would enjoy for a long time her gratitude and approval. Etol also owed me a few favors. I shrugged and carried the necklace back to my furs. My head ached but there was no place to get away from Crane's shrieking baby. The child expressed all our emotions. We let him scream. Really, the lodge *was* too crowded.

The next morning Etol started to build our tent and Chi motioned that he wanted to talk privately. We had not walked far when my son faced me. In his winter clothes, he seemed big and wide. His mouth, pushed slightly out, reminded me of Jak. Yes, the way he held his arms and straightened his shoulders was much like his father. Chi had Jak's way of appearing larger than he was. Last night Crane had also made me think of my first husband. The three of them shared the same lineage. None of this put me in a good mood.

"You know why I offered Crane the necklace," I jumped in before Chi could speak.

My son looked startled. He had not meant to talk directly about the necklace. He wanted to begin with more general complaints.

"You do not," Chi struggled so that I felt sorry for him, "value . . . that gift. It took me a winter. It was the tusk of the matriarch."

"I know," I answered as nicely as I could. "And I have it still. I value it very much."

"You gave it away."

"To prevent your aunt from leaving, to keep with us your uncle and cousins and all the children born to them."

Unexpectedly I found a way to talk to Chi about his marriage. Children make us strong, and I was anxious for Chi to have children of his own. I had a new thought. My sister was in my debt. Surely now, Sage would relent about the girl in the lodge next to ours. Chi should go immediately to that lodge. He should insist!

"You do not want some people to leave our camp," my son responded bitterly, "but you want me to leave."

I did not pay much attention to this. For too long I had felt guilty about Chi. I could not take away the scars on his shoulder or the years we quarreled. I could not change the way he hunted ivory. But I could help my son get children who would press their skin against his skin, who would touch him for comfort and take away his loneliness.

"You must ask for the girl with the new tattoo," I said. "Perhaps the husband of Dipper's daughter will go with you."

"I do not want to live with that . . . family," Chi stuttered.

"What do you know?" I shouted suddenly. "You are a man now. Behave like a man!"

"Then I *will* go away," my son replied in rage. "You want me to go and I *will*."

This is how some winters end, no matter how hard we try. This is what we fear, living so close together, wet and cold, bored and hungry. We want fresh green food and a fresh green life. We hate the smoke that hurts our eyes and we hate the dirty shoes drying over the fire. I had done my best to keep tied to this camp my brother and sister-in-law, a man and woman I did not even like. Then I lost my temper and caused my son to leave.

That very morning, Chi took his weapons and disappeared.
I could not even imagine what Sage would say.

Chapter Nine

We moved from the lodge to one of our camps, and still Chi did not return. I hoped he had gone to visit that girl's family, who would also be leaving their winter lodge. Finally the husbands of Dipper's daughter and Crane's daughter said they would take me to see their parents. For four days we walked to reach an empty camp, long unused. A pile of old hides, half eaten by mice, lay on the ground. Blue jays screeched angrily nearby. The two men shrugged. Their group must have chosen another place, farther west, by a stream that flowed even in this drought.

We walked another day and I felt excited to see the shapes of hills I had never seen before. Curiously this land poked at my eyes and ears, wanting to know my story, anxious to please me. I praised its jumbles of rock and distant mountains purple and lavender. Twisted cholla stood up like women gesturing with their arms. Among the mesquite, I found a flower with pink petals around a green center. This was a new flower, and I wondered what it could do. Along the way we hunted small game, which seemed to be plentiful.

"What are you looking for?" the land whispered, flat and rolling, pink and yellow. "Come here, here, here, tell me everything."

The husband of Crane's daughter smelled smoke in the wind and said, smiling, that this was smoke from his family's fire. Approaching the camp, we saw three women cooking skewers of freshly caught fish. Like blue jays they also cried an alarm before they recognized us. Then the woman with flint under her skin embraced her sons and greeted me as though I were her sister. With her daughters, she prepared a feast to celebrate our visit—cakes ground from seed, boiled salad, antelope, and tapir. The fruit of the prickly pear was not yet ripe but these people made another sweet jam out of roots. They told us to sit and served generously.

I felt envious. This was an even larger group than ours, with plenty of adults to hunt and gather. Near the stream, I counted ten tents, each one made of camel hides covered with patterns—red for blood, yellow for sun, white for spirit. I wondered if Sage knew about these dyes. I wondered if we could draw these circles and lines on our tents.

Shyly I did not even ask about the girl with the new tattoo. I could see many children playing, many girls. But I no longer cared about that. For all my time here, the woman who works stone gave me food and I ate without pleasure. Chi had not come to see this family after all.

We had walked for five days and the husbands naturally

wanted to stay with their relatives to rest and gossip. I hurried them back sooner than they liked. If my son was not with this group, he would surely be at the spring gathering. To reach that gathering, we had to travel fast, jogging steadily through the pink-and-yellow land. Our legs ached at night and the two men became annoyed with me. Hoping to make peace, I did most of the cooking and promised my help if ever they needed it around the central fire.

Late one afternoon we saw the flaps of our tents, undecorated and shabby. Our family had waited for our return.

The very next morning, we all packed up and began walking to reach the narrow-leafed trees by the big river. Crane and Vole were eager to find husbands for their last two daughters, long past their monthly blood. Etol was less eager to be at this gathering for he feared his sons had grown tired waiting for Wolf's stepdaughters to become their wives. He worried they would find someone else to marry. I reassured him. No one wanted a son-in-law without gifts from the parents. More important, Etol's sons wanted to stay with us.

I remembered that Chi had also wanted to stay. I promised myself I would greet him without reproach. If he did not choose to marry this spring, I would not insist.

Of course I hoped he had changed his mind. Pleasant stories filled my thoughts on the long walk over the mountains. First I imagined a girl whose family had died or abandoned her, someone who would come to us with tears and gratitude. Then I realized that such a trauma was too big. The girl would be damaged. So I saw my son with a woman like Wolf's wife, a husband she did not like, a poor hunter or a man with a bad temper. Perhaps the husband was dead. That would be better. Now I saw a widow with a baby girl. That child could become the wife of the son of Crane's daughter. Perhaps this woman even had two girls! Another wife for the son of Dipper's daughter or for the son of Crane herself, the little boy who had teethed on my ivory necklace. I saw our family grow even stronger, tied together in trust and blood.

We found the spring gathering by walking the ridges and looking for smoke. That year, the gathering was small, to the north, at a bend in the river.

Chi was not there.

The men from two other families danced in a circle around the fire, and Crane stood and judged them, watching their muscles move under their skin, watching their genitals flap. One man, as old as Etol, was interested in joining our family group. Then Crane's sons-in-law took another hunter aside and spoke to him persuasively. So Crane's two girls finally got husbands. Etol's boys went hunting for a black bear they had seen tearing up a log. They came back happy with a new bearskin. No one was hurt. No one fought. For everyone but me, the gathering was a success.

On our return to the summer camp, I followed Sage's braid, black and gray, swinging over the hump of her leather pack. We passed the place where hills lie down like sleeping animals. We passed two breasts covered with sweet grass, an outcropping on one like an aroused nipple. The men made their jokes but I did not smile and I did not hunt with them. Sage's braid moved restlessly as she walked. I knew that my son was still alive. I believed that my sister and I would have felt his death.

But where was he?

When I was a child, a man-beast once came to one of our gatherings. Bleeding from the nose and very dirty, he stumbled down a pile of rocks, looking for a healer. He walked awkwardly, for his shoulder had been twisted in a bad fall. At the campfire, my father spoke of him with compassion. This was a boy from my father's own lineage.

"A man-beast is someone who lives alone," my father said, "like a badger or short-faced bear, in a cave or shelter, hunting only for himself, talking only to himself, or not talking at all."

I leaned against the warmth of my father's arm. "How long does a man-beast live?" I asked. I did not see how anyone could survive without a family group. Hunting alone was always dangerous. Without help, even a small injury could be deadly.

"Some die very soon." My father nodded. "Others stay alive for a long time. You see, they're man-beasts. They think like animals but they are cleverer than animals. They are strong, quick, good with a club, good with a spear. They do nothing but sleep, eat, hunt. Some of them no longer cook their meat. Some of them no longer speak our language. If you ever see a man-beast, Willow, run away as fast as you can."

This made me want to see a man-beast more than ever. Boldly, with another boy from another camp, I went to play near the healer's tent, where I knew the man-beast slept inside. Urging each other on, the boy and I crept nearer to the closed flap. Quickly I pulled aside one corner and peeked in.

Lying naked on his side, the man-beast startled awake. His face and body looked the same as any other man's but his eyes were rounder and wetter, like the eyes of an otter. They seemed to shine in the half-light of the tent. As he rose up on one arm and tried to stand, he began to roar, not words at all but a garbled sound with only parts of words. I had never seen anyone so full of fear.

Terrified, I did just what my father told me to do. I ran away as fast as I could. I never knew what happened to the boy I was with and I never saw him again. For the rest of that gathering, I stayed close to my mother and sister.

Years later, when I was first hunting with Etol and Golden, we found the body of a man-beast, dead for many winters, his bones dirty white on the yellow plain. Squatting together, we talked for some time about whether we should bury these bones like the bones of a human or leave them like the bones of an animal. Golden wanted to dig a grave. Etol and I disagreed.

"Some people say that man-beasts finally turn into animals," Etol said. "We should leave these things here as we would leave a horse or buffalo."

Golden picked up the man's skull. "He is not an animal yet."

"Perhaps he was not a man-beast long enough," I suggested. "Still, he made this choice. We should respect that."

"Some people say that man-beasts came to this land even before Tewa and Tono." Etol spoke like an elder, a role he would try on from time to time, although my cousin and I did our best to discourage it. "Some of these man-beasts turned into the fathers of the animals here. To treat a man-beast like a human is wrong. They are not the same."

Golden was never a person who liked to argue. With a shrug, he put down the man-beast's skull, and we walked away, eager to keep hunting. I did not say a single prayer to the bones on the ground. Instead, I felt contempt. Only a fool would want to live alone.

I let my senses spread thin, making a net thin enough to catch an antelope, a fat horse, a young camel.

Up until this very day, following Sage's braid, I had never thought about that man-beast again. Now it was Chi I saw stumbling from the rocks with his face dirty and hair matted. Eventually he would stop speaking to himself and his thoughts would be animal thoughts, wordless knowledge. I saw him in a cave, a man-beast without a mother or friend, without a healer to help him when he was hurt. To stay alive would be difficult, more challenging than before. Probably Chi would like that. He would forget his love of ivory and simply stay alive. Perhaps after many years, he would turn into a lion and the scars on his shoulder would no longer hurt when he stretched back his arm. I thought back to that night long ago by the river near the bluff. Something had entered my son in the lion's bite. Something gnawed at him, close to the heart. Now he would become a man-beast. He would become that skull on the ground. When he died no one would put red ochre on his bones.

I had never felt so tired. For too many days I had been traveling, walking, first to the camp of Dipper's husband's people, then to the gathering, now back to our camp. Sometimes I turned feverish and broke into a sweat. I knew I should go to Crane for help but I did not want to hear the triumph in her voice. Wearily I followed the gray and black of my sister's braid. Stubbornly I reached my tent and crawled into it. There I slept and dreamed and ignored Etol's questions. That was the beginning of everything else. That was when I lost my monthly blood.

Like a mean husband, Old Man continued to watch us too closely. His bright eye rose each day, red, yellow, white, burning, asking—what will you do now?

In the places where springs still flowed from the ground, we left spear points of chert and quartz. These were large points no hunter would ever use. They were meant as offerings. In the riverbed, we dug wells. The men did most of the work, their dark arms and chests gleaming. We women lowered the gourds with yucca rope to reach the muddy water below. No one in our group ever went thirsty.

When we hunted, however, we saw how much the animals suffered. Their ribs could be counted, one by one. They moved slowly. Their bony bodies had hardly any fat.

Because we craved fat ourselves, we began eating the pocket of grease behind each animal's eyeball. In any carcass, camel, horse, or deer, we cracked the bones for their marrow. Now we cracked all the bones we could find, scattered on the ground or at a kill.

By pools of shallow water, we saw odd groups, lions and tapirs, dire wolves and llamas, foxes and rabbits. We saw rare animals like the mastodon and shy ones like the little spotted cat. In the drying mud, the tracks crossed and criss-crossed, giant insect-eaters, giant sloths, peccaries, beavers, porcupines, skunks, bears, cheetahs, coyotes, voles, mice, raccoons, waterbirds. Often we walked up to our weakened prey and killed them just to eat that little bit of grease at the back of their eyes.

Whenever we could, we also killed mammoths for the cushiony fat in their feet and trunk, for their ivory and for the glory that still remained, the pleasure of bringing home mammoth meat. The mammoths themselves moved restlessly across the plain. Etol saw Red Fur leading her herd high into the spruce forests. I saw other places too where the animals had killed tree after tree by stripping away bark and rising up on their hind legs to get the last branch, the last leaf or needle.

For most of that summer, Sage and I avoided each other. Privately, differently, we grieved for Chi. My stories about him kept changing. Sometimes he was a man-beast. Sometimes he traveled to the south, an explorer like Tono driven to see places he had never seen. Sometimes he was injured, taken in by a family and nursed by a girl with a new tattoo.

That other thing was happening to me too. Since the beginning of winter, I had not had my blood. There had been times like this before, but never for so long. Often I felt hot again, drenched in sweat. At night I could not sleep. When I did, my dreams woke me. My heart pounded as though I had been dreaming of a dance and shaman's drum.

At last one afternoon, as we gathered the seeds of feather grass, I spoke to Sage. I knew what she would say and still I wanted to protest. I was not ready.

"We'll do it tomorrow when the eye of Old Woman is open." Sage shook a clump of grass into the basket, let the stems rise, and reached for another handful. "Otherwise you will have to wait a month."

"I can wait," I replied. On this I felt firm, and firmly I also bent a handful of grass into my gathering basket and shook the stems so the seeds fell rustling to the bottom.

"Tomorrow." Sage did not pause in her work.

Suddenly I saw my mother's face again. I remembered how she had looked when we gathered seeds together. Just as Mother tattooed women for their first blood, so she tattooed them for their last blood. Now Sage wanted to do my tattoo on a night when Old Woman could watch and help.

"It will hurt," I said childishly.

Sage laughed. "No one welcomes this mark as much as the first one." She shook her grass.

"But look." She turned so that I could see her naked thighs. Below each buttock, two cat claws raked the skin. She was a completed woman. "I have never had children. Even so I gave all my blood to our people. Most women die with blood inside them, but I gave all I had and I am glad of that. You will feel the same. You will also be a completed woman, a generous woman."

Sage's small breasts jiggled when she faced me again. Her breasts still looked young, breasts that had never been nursed or pulled by careless hands. I reached down to touch the scars on my leg. I had never thought of myself as unfinished. I felt the smoothness of my other thigh.

The next night, under a yellow moon, I lay on the ground while my sister cut my leg with an obsidian flake. The eye of Old Woman silvered the rocks in this small clearing, near enough camp to be safe, far enough to be private. Resting my forehead on the dirt, I felt the pebbles and thorns under my stomach. On my unmarked leg, Sage drew three wavy lines, the sign for being female, a common tattoo. The marks were as long as my hand and she cut deeply. Then she rubbed in dye that burned like stinging nettle. When I was young, the first time, I refused to make a sound. Now I yelped.

"Shhh!" Sage scolded. "It's almost over."

The marks of a tattoo are carefully watched and rarely become infected. Even so Sage made certain prayers and I left an offering of blue stone to the silver moon. It is hard, sometimes, for us to know what is expected, what we must do to keep ourselves safe. We only know that this is a dangerous world. So we do everything we can.

By the central fire, Etol gossiped. As I limped into our tent, he called for me to join him. In a few moments, annoyed, he came to the tent himself. I showed him my thigh with its caked blood.

"Huh!" He was surprised. "You didn't tell me about this."

"Do you tell me everything?" I was annoyed too.

My husband lay down as though to sleep. After a pause, he spoke again. "So you are a generous woman now."

I smiled into the darkness. "I will be generous," I promised, "when my leg heals."

I knew what Etol would say next.

"Generous women are good for hunting."

It is an old hunter's saying.

That summer, the dry dusty days were like the dryness in my body, drained of its blood. I did not feel the same. I was like a child but I was not a child. I would never have children again, and I did not have children now in this camp. Everything about my life seemed old, like the earth, like the dying water holes. Everything seemed vague and unimportant—except for the pain of the three lines in my leg. They hurt the most when I squatted to work or relieve myself. They hurt when I hurried through the yellow grass or rolled over in my sleep. They healed slowly, leaving three raised dark brown scars.

Slowly, too, I began to feel better. I was a completed woman. My dry body seemed lighter than before. My mother had died at Wolf's birth and I have seen others die the same way, growing weaker and sadder, their blood soaking through the pads of moss, their hands loosening in the midwife's hand. Sometimes babies are trapped in the mother's body, and then she screams with pain and frustration, everyone dying. These memories come to women as they lie with men. These memories have lived in my tent and in my bed. Now the weight of that death was gone.

Other burdens dropped away. I no longer had to gather grass for my flow or bathe in the cold winter or say no to my husband because of the blood. My work was finished. Sage was right. When I walked, my thighs flashed their twin marks, six lines rippling, three on each side. Young women do not know this feeling of pride. I saw that we older ones do not talk about it.

I did feel more generous too. With Chi gone, Etol and I were alone in our tent in the flickering light. We could be as tender or as playful as we wished. Etol forgot how I had once lived apart from him, his wife but not his wife. I forgot that afternoon with the snowflakes in the air, when he walked away knowing I would follow. Now we talked easily about Jak and Dipper, about Etol's two sons and daughter, about his grandchildren and their marriages. I even spoke to my husband of his sister, Crane. At last we came to each other for advice.

More generously I went to Crane's daughter and Dipper's daughter and took their children so that the mothers could go into the forest or field. More often, Wolf's wife brought me her twins. Their crinkly eyes made me smile as I pressed my lips to their soft skin and blew lightly into the navel. My old woman's breath would strengthen their lungs. I held them and let them go back to their mothers. I let go the bones of little Crow, the memory of Ali, of my son, Chi, back to the earth with my blood. I released my grip and found in my hand thorns and pebbles, bits of grass, stems, and flowers.

In the darkness I continued to dream strangely. One night as I lay awake, the matriarch's necklace of ivory beads whispered low so that Ftol could not hear. I crept over to the far side of the tent where the necklace was wrapped in moss and deerskin. Amazed, frightened, I put my ear next to the bundle.

"So you are dry like me," the matriarch said, "and now you can hear me and I have someone to talk to, someone who will listen to my stories.

"I owe you a debt," the matriarch said. "The sight of my favorite son lying dead filled me with rage. I saw red from the blood in my eyes and I wanted that red to be your husband's heart. When the grass parted to show his face, I knew he was hiding and I tricked him into lying still like a fawn. I wanted to open him as he had opened my son. I wanted to wait for his flesh to fall away so I could scatter his bones across the plain. As I trampled his body, I felt his death under my feet. My anger left me then. I was wrong to kill your husband like that.

"I will tell you about sweet grass," the matriarch said. "The sweet grass of spring believes it will reach the face of Old Man and it grows and grows, climbing up to the sky while its roots reach down to anchor it against the moment when its stalk touches Old Man's body. As we eat the grass, the dream in the grass becomes our dream and the heat of Old

Man fills our stomach and we wait for the time when we will stop eating Old Man and we will become Old Man, when a white light will run through us, the light of the sun.

"I will tell you about feather grass. . . . "

Fascinated, I listened to the secrets of the mammoth herd. The matriarch especially liked to talk about the plants she had eaten, and her stories about grass were long and mysterious like the stories of a shaman. At the same time, she could be practical—in the details of where the best grass grew and at what season. Listening, I learned many things to tell Sage.

One afternoon at the end of summer, as I sat and wove a loose willow basket, Etol's sons come rushing up the trail from the dry riverbed. They had left the morning before with Etol and Wolf in a hunting party we thought would be gone many days. The men breathed heavily for they had been running, carrying their spears, their empty packs flapping.

"Hello, little wife," one of them gasped to the girl near my feet. This was Wolf's stepdaughter, who squirmed in delight and embarrassment. In a few winters, she would be this man's wife. Still I shook my head. His words were early.

"Mother," the same man said to me because he was polite and liked to call me that. "Chi has returned!"

I let go of the willow basket.

"He's well," Etol's son assured me, "and he has brought guests."

Now I will cook food, I thought. I understood why Etol had sent his sons ahead. I had time to make a feast.

"Sage!" I called.

"Golden is with him," Etol's son continued, his breath still coming hard. "Golden and his wife and three children. And Ali is with him too! Ali and her children, two girls, twins!"

But this was a story I had never told myself. Dazed, I picked up my unfinished basket, the strips of snowy white trailing on the ground. Everything I ever knew left me. I could not think of what food to prepare. My hands clutched the basket tighter. Fortunately my sister hurried to my side. Willingly she did all the work.

When I let my daughter go to the shaman's camp, I knew I would never see her again. Sage may have hoped at each spring gathering but I never did. I never saw the two halves join. In a way I was right. The woman who walked beside Chi now was not the girl who had left me in my tent. Surprisingly, that girl had gone backward in time, split into two younger girls running beside the grown-up Ali. Now there were four halves, and each one a stranger, even the one I called myself. I could not talk. I could not think.

Oh, I was happy to see Ali and my new granddaughters. I was happy to see Chi and his triumph at bringing me this gift, so much better—he seemed to boast—than a daughter-in-law!

But I felt confused, perhaps because I had never expected this happiness. It was like giving birth. But at birth, everything is clear. The baby suckles the breast. The need we have for each other is clear.

I must have seemed like a crazy woman, holding my unfinished basket as though it were a charm or child's toy. I could not look directly at my daughter. Sideways, glancing, I saw different parts—an arm, a leg, a long scar on her face from cheek to chin.

Sage knew better what to do. My sister took Ali to the clearing where she had given me my second tattoo. I followed silently. Now my other half would speak.

Chapter Ten

"When I went to the shaman's camp and left my mother in her tent, I thought I would see her at the next spring gathering. I did not want to leave my family. I was being taken by the bear. I saw something in Old Woman I had never seen before and she took me to the bear because she saw something in me she had never seen before. She said I was strong. She said I was ready.

"No, Old Woman did not speak. Tireus, my husband's wife, said this. She flattered me and I felt important. When Tireus left me alone with the shaman, I desired a man for the first time. When he put his hands on me, I burned in the light of Old Woman. The heat of that made me strong enough to leave. I never thought I would be gone this long.

"Of course I was glad that Golden and Tit decided to join us. With our new family group, we traveled south. It was exciting to see hills shaped differently! With Tireus at my side, I began to find new plants. My husband's wife showed me which ones to pick for food, for medicine, for color, for smell. The other women were also friendly and the shaman was kind when we mated at night.

"Even so, I missed my mother and aunt. Then I went to Golden or Tit and we planned how we would surprise you in the spring with gifts from this land. Golden especially made me feel good because he felt good, grinning when he thought of his new wife. His eyes met mine and we looked away. We all lived in the fever of Old Man humping Old Woman.

"As we traveled, I began to understand that the shaman's people lived far from the spring gathering, much farther than I had thought. Tireus explained that the shaman had wanted a second wife from the north. He wanted more children from the north. Tireus was older than her husband and had given him three sons before she became a completed woman. 'The bear chose me when he was still a boy,' my co-wife said proudly. 'I left my first marriage for him. Like you, I left my family group.' After that, Tireus and I were like two sisters. She shared everything with me, everything she knew.

"At night, with the shaman, I waited to see the bear again, big and shaggy. But my husband seemed to behave like any other man, quick and pleased to be with me. We mated and touched each other for comfort. Then we slept, tired from traveling so far and fast.

"I walked beside my husband for a long time before we came to a camp by a shallow lake. Water stretched out as far as I could see so that the water looked like gray land. This disturbed me. Every morning as the sun came up, the noise of birds filled the air and the sky filled with bodies swirling in clouds that blocked the light. Honking, calling to each other, the birds rose from the lake to feed on marshes nearby. I never really became used to this noise.

"I should tell you now what we ate. Whenever we wanted, we roasted waterbirds, a wonderful greasy meat. In the spring, we gathered baskets of eggs that the women cooked on a central fire. We also found plants with glossy leaves and crunchy roots as big as my hand. All year round we ate fish and turtles. In the fall and winter, the men hunted animals who came to drink and bathe at the lake. The hunters killed these animals without much trouble. This was good because we had a lot of people to feed. The shaman led a group so large his camp seemed more like a gathering than a family.

"Soon after we arrived, Golden and Tit went to live at another part of the lake, near the mother of their wives, and I saw them less often. I lived with the shaman, Tireus, their three sons, and their sons' families. One morning I woke and felt as though I had been sleeping for a long time. I was surrounded by strangers, a second wife in a land of water. My face, arms, legs, and chest, even my crotch, were infected with mosquito bites. The bites became sores, scabby and crusted. Whenever she missed me, Tireus came to look by the central fire, where I sat red-eyed in the smoke. Every summer and spring, the mosquitoes plagued me. In the winter they left, and I had some peace.

"By the second spring I understood that the shaman was not going to take me back to see my family. My husband made promises that he meant at the time but might not mean later, for he was ruled always by the moods of the bear. He was a handsome man—you have seen him—with thick hair and a hunter's tattoo under the nipple of his breast. In many ways he was good to me, gentle at night, gentle with Tireus and his grandchildren. As his wife, I became wealthy. People gave us gifts when he tranced and told the future. I had a dress covered with white feathers tied by a belt of red, orange, and green. I had a necklace of pink shells. I had more skins than I could tan.

"By the second spring I was also pregnant, and I had seen my husband trance many times. Most often the spittle fell from his mouth, his hands curved into claws, and his eyes rolled back until he dropped to the ground. Sometimes the fury of the short-faced bear made him crawl instead, on his arms and legs, roaring and snarling so that fear held us still. Sometimes he would leap at a man or woman, smashing them with his shaggy paws like the giant bear smashes its prey. Terrified, the people would cower, too afraid to run, yet unwilling to fight back. The next day, the bruises on their faces would show dark and their arms would be bloody from scratches. Still they had no shame, and my husband had no shame. He was ruled by the bear who honored the lake people by coming among them, even when he smashed them to the ground.

"My first child, a girl, was born dead with two loops of purple cord around her neck. Tireus and I wept and held each other and the shaman was as sorry as we were. Later he came at night to be with me. I saw his tears when he rubbed the tiny body, so small and well formed, with red ochre. Because she was his daughter, the people weighted her with stones and put her in the lake. The fish ate her and we ate the fish.

"Early the next summer my second child, another girl, was also born dead. Again the purple cord had strangled her in the womb. This time I screamed and hit the shaman with my fists, hitting the muscles of his chest like I was hitting a drum. In his anger at the loss of his child, he began to rear up, and Tireus cried out, 'No, not here!' and he mewled like a cub and ran away. Again we rubbed the little body with red ochre and put her in the lake.

"After this, other children died. A boy drowned. A snake bit Tit's new daughter. My husband said that Old Woman was punishing us, although he did not know why. His eyes rolled back and he tranced often, searching for an answer. Some of the people blamed me. Some of them blamed Tireus. Another child never woke in the morning for no reason we could see, and this was Tireus's own grandson. She wailed like a white waterbird.

"Now I will tell you that these people do not move to a winter lodge, but at that time of year, when it is cold and they are tired of fish, rain, and sleet, they also become irritable. More than ever I wanted to return to my mother, but I did not know the way—and Golden would not help me.

"Soon I found myself pregnant again. This time I was very big and uncomfortable. To everyone's surprise I had twins, both girls, and they both lived.

"Finally the lake people accepted me. I had added to their lineage and given them twins, which they thought lucky. Even the mosquitoes seemed to bother me less. Like Tireus, I simply covered myself with mud and went about dirty. I had plenty to do with two babies. At last, I was happy.

"Only my husband did not see that our lives were good. He insisted that Old Woman was still angry. At night he dreamed of our dead children, whose spirits, he said, cried to him from the gray lake. They called out in a rush of noise flying up like birds, without the bodies of birds, a horrible sound. After these dreams, he feared for the lives of our new baby girls and he would often stand over them, whispering to himself.

"One day when the twins were old enough to sit beside Tireus, he said that she could not touch them. She could not speak to them. He tore them from her hands even as they cried and she cried and I cried. From then on, Tireus had to sleep in another tent, away from me and the shaman. He said that she was dangerous. In a low voice, as if afraid she might overhear, he asked me to describe the births of our first and second child. What had Tireus been doing?

Had I seen the babies myself? Where did she take the purple cords?

"Alarmed, Tireus and I kept this a secret from the other lake people. Sometimes for long periods, the shaman seemed to forget these ideas, and he would invite Tireus to come eat with us, smiling at her warmly. Still he did not like her sitting too close. Whenever I could, I went to my co-wife and tried to comfort her. But what could I say? Neither of us understood what was happening.

"Alone in our tent, the shaman was still a gentle man. But now he said it was wrong for us to mate.

"Outside the tent, he continued to lead the people, and most of his decisions were good. Only sometimes they were not. Sometimes they were bad. When he tranced, the mood of the bear was unpredictable. Once my husband picked up a full-grown man, held him in the air, and threw him to the ground. Once he bit a child on the cheek. The next day, he was frightened. 'Why would Old Woman punish a child?' he asked me. 'Now she has blood all over her face.' He pointed at the sun. 'Can you see it?'

"When the moon was full, one bright night, the shaman grew into the shape of the giant short-faced bear and his sharp teeth clicked as he reared up high on his hind legs. His thick black hair swung when he roared. Snarling, he swiped at the air with his paws. I had never seen him grow so big. I had never felt so afraid.

"Suddenly he rushed at Tireus, who stood apart by herself. He rushed at his wife and circled his hands around her throat and began to squeeze. In a second he was no longer a bear but just a man killing a woman. He muttered the same thing over and over with no pause between the words and no sense in their meaning.

"At first none of us moved. He was the shaman. He was the bear. Then Tireus's sons came forward and tried to break their father's grip. But my husband had very strong hands. Even as the men pulled at his arms, those hands crushed Tireus's throat. In front of us all, without protest, she died. Blood spurted from her mouth, and her head flopped against her shoulder.

"When the shaman collapsed, a woman screamed. Afterward they said it was the bear who killed Tireus. Some said they saw the face of Old Woman covered by a red cloud. I did not believe any of this. I saw the spirit of the bear leave the shaman as soon as he began to strangle his first wife. I saw my husband kill my friend, my sister, and when I could think clearly I knew I could no longer stay by the lake where they threw in Tireus's body. The bones of my children lay at the bottom to keep her company. That was all I could give my co-wife.

"At the burial, as they weighted Tireus with stones, the shaman guessed what I meant to do. 'Do you want to go?' he asked me, his eyes wet with tears. His voice was soft.

"I answered no and touched the shoulders of my two girls, strong girls big enough to travel.

"Even so, the shaman watched me closely through the

rest of that summer, fall, and winter. I was not impatient. I needed time to think about how to leave, how to convince Golden to come with me.

I did not try to talk to Tit, who had three wives now and many children. Tit knew more than the lake people about killing mammoths and he had become famous among their hunters. When I saw my cousin at a distance, I often thought he was a lake man himself with his cape of white feathers and long fishing spear. When we came together, face to face, I stared at the cane plug in his nose, the mark of certain people who do secret things on an island in the lake. I did not go to Tit because I knew what he would say and I was afraid he would tell the shaman. I had the same fears about Golden. Regretfully I remembered our long walk from the spring gathering. I wished I had paid more attention then. I knew I could not find my way back alone.

"These lake people take wives easily. Golden's second wife was a barren woman he married as a favor to my husband. Her leg bent from an old injury and her voice could be heard a great distance. Still she was a powerful person, with a piece of cane as big as a finger in her nose. Before and after she went to the secret island, this wife demanded a lot of attention. Golden's first wife had already given birth to two girls. Her youngest was a boy in her arms. Even so, she had to massage the second wife's feet, cook and bring her food, sew her clothing, and tan her skins. Often we heard that second wife across the camp, scolding the first wife and complaining about her children. This always made me glad. If the people in Golden's tent were unhappy, maybe he would be willing to leave them.

"One afternoon after gathering sedge, I saw my cousin alone with his youngest daughter, dragging a soft-shell turtle spitted on a branch. The people of the lake used this path often, and it was safe from animals—but not from gossip. I kept my voice low. Quietly I asked Golden why he was so cruel.

"He looked surprised. I reminded him of his mother and father. Surely they longed to see their son? We had promised to return at the next spring gathering. Now many years had passed. What had they done to deserve his hatred?

"Still surprised, Golden protested. He did not hate his parents. He thought of them often.

"I put my hand on his daughter's hair. 'How are your wives?' I asked carefully.

"My cousin knew what I meant. 'Go ahead of us,' he told his daughter. I understood from his voice that he would never leave her. Obediently the girl took the turtle, which was still alive, its hind claws digging into the earth. 'How is the shaman?' Golden asked.

"'You saw what he did!' I started to cry.

"My cousin tried to calm me. 'That was in the summer,' he said. 'That was the bear.'

"My face showed my feelings.

"Golden sighed and looked at the ground.

"'I am afraid.' I spoke quickly for I heard another lake man singing as he walked along the path. 'I am afraid for myself and for my children, who are from your lineage too, from your mother's lineage. Talk to your first wife, Golden,' I begged. 'Ask her if she is willing to leave here and go north to our family group.'

"A month later, we did not find it so hard. The shaman had tranced and fallen into a sleep that would last through the night and next day. When he woke, he would be confused. Golden's second wife also slept deeply for different reasons, a medicine I had learned from Tireus. As we crept away from the lake, Golden's first wife carried the baby while her two girls and my twins walked behind. Anxiously we warned the children to be quiet, as silent as though we were on a hunt. Once away from camp, we drove them without mercy, shaming them whenever they stumbled or complained.

"In case my husband followed, Golden did not take us directly north. Instead we went up a small stream that fed into the lake. The water wet our clothes and washed away our tracks. In the starlight, I carried a spear and watched for animals.

"'Do you think he will come after us?' the first wife asked.

"'I don't know,' I answered honestly. 'I think he has grown tired of me. I think he has grown tired of many things.'

"Strangely, I felt sad leaving the man who had taken me from my family, the father of my children, the murderer of Tireus. I could no longer remember why I had left my mother's tent. But I saw again how my husband had wept when our babies died.

"Under the eye of Old Man, we traveled fast and we were lucky. Nothing attacked us. We found a dead stallion for food.

"Then, from a distance, my brother, Chi, saw our group struggle across the plain with more children than adults. Even now I do not understand why he came down to speak with us. Why would Chi talk to strangers? And why was he alone without his family group?

"Chi would not tell me—which is exactly how I remember him. We stared at each other like two buffalo calves, big-eyed and wobbly. Then we began to laugh with relief! Golden and I laughed too, knowing we had been right to make this journey. Our children laughed as well because that is what everyone else was doing, even the baby in the first wife's arms."

Ali told her story to Sage and me, and then she told it with a few changes to all the adults around the central fire. We listened greedily. The people of the lake intrigued us with their feathers and fish and waterbirds. Especially we wanted to hear about the shaman. Vole and I could remember when our uncle's uncle had tranced to tell the future. But we had never had a bear live among us as a husband and father.

I wept when I heard how Ali had suffered, my other half, the other mother I had been. Why did the giant short-faced bear stalk us?

Ali cried when she heard about Crow, Dipper, and Second Crow.

"Was that the shaman?" I whispered.

"No!" she said in horror. "He was not like that. You do not understand."

"How did you get that scar," Sage asked, "across your face?"

"A branch," Ali said. "Tireus and I were gathering herbs for the pain of old people in their hands. I made a joke and Tireus pretended to run from me. She could run like a girl! I chased her although I was big with child and a branch struck me across the face. It was not deep but it left a scar. I chased her still, covering her with the pollen of a cattail. That was the joke, to make her fertile again."

Ali smiled at the memory, and Sage smiled back, happy to hear something good from the lake of waterbirds.

"And the herb?" my sister wondered.

Ali shook her head. "It does not grow here."

Secretly I felt sore inside. I was jealous thinking of the blood on my daughter's face, the older woman turning to smile, the white fluff of cattails. She could run like a girl! In Tireus's tent, two babies were born, two babies died, my daughter beat the shaman's chest, and two babies were covered with red ochre. So many important things happened without me.

My cousin Golden had his own story, and the wife he brought with him also spoke, softly at first, then boldly as she ate our camel meat. She was a strong woman to leave her people because she did not like her co-wife. Sage and I glanced at each other. We did not want another strong woman like Crane. In this, as you know, we were wrong.

Sitting next to their mother, Golden's two girls looked plump and healthy, with clear skin and white milk teeth. Golden showed them off proudly, saying their names for us. At this, Vole frowned. But my cousin was right to keep for his children the names given by the people of the lake.

For Golden, this homecoming was not what he had expected. His mother, father, sister, and nephew were dead. New husbands and wives sat across from him at the central fire. Now he must have mourned Tit, his only brother, living far away and angry at him for leaving. As Golden talked, I hummed my approval, saying without words, "I am here." Etol also murmured and reached out to touch Golden's arm, saying without words, "I am here. We will hunt together soon."

Golden made the best of things. He was always a cheerful man who liked to please people. "I missed this land," he told us loudly so that the land would hear. "I missed this summer camp with the hill above us shaped like a tooth. You can not imagine the mosquitoes I lived with by that ugly lake. Mosquitoes as big . . . as buffalo."

Next to Ali, my new granddaughters giggled. I could not stop staring at them, the thick black hair, the eyes like the oval seeds of a cactus, the giggle lines crinkling smooth brown skin. They looked just alike. They looked like Ali, only their mouths twisted up, the top lip jutting. That came from the shaman.

Without fear, my granddaughters also stared at me, for they felt the gaze of my curious love. They felt my love brushing their cheeks and smoothing their hair. Ali must have told them good stories because from our first meeting they loved me too. Yes, from their first night in camp, they came to me whenever they felt lonely, knowing I would be more patient than their mother. Ali felt bad about taking her chil- dren so far from their home, and she would not listen to her daughters talk about the lake of waterbirds. But I listened gratefully. For each story they told me, I told them one of mine. I told them about their new family, the people of the hill shaped like a tooth, the descendants of brave Tewa and Tono.

At the beginning of fall, the rains came late and flowers bloomed suddenly, past their time. The cones of the piñon pine bulged and the branches of juniper sagged under the weight of hard purple berries. The oak trees suffered, battered by bears and other animals looking for acorns. We would gather them also to grind into mush.

"Grandmother, put this on!" the twins commanded me, holding up a string of yellow daisies. I looped the necklace over my head and praised their wreaths, yellow flowers twined in the thick black hair, flowers puffing out their chests like breasts.

"How pretty!" I said. "Now I look pretty too."

From Sage's tent, my daughter Ali walked over carrying a pack. She meant to go gathering and wanted the girls to help her strip the leaves and bring home a load.

When they pouted, she looked annoyed.

"I remember bringing you flowers," she said to me.

"They were beautiful," I agreed.

Ali shook her head. "You were busy then, like I am."

"No," I insisted. "Our tent was always full of flowers. We crumpled them in the fire to make a good smell."

"I'm in a hurry now," my daughter said, walking on, half pleased, half scolding.

The petals tickled my cheek like fingers. Pale yellow can be the color of Old Woman and white-yellow the color of Old Man. These flowers were brighter, a color I could hear as well as see. Straining, I tried to listen.

Yellow tangled my granddaughters' hair. Chi was home. Ali was home. This is a moment I carry in my bones. Orange pollen smudged my granddaughter's nose. Now the same orange dusted my cheek. Joy, the pollen whispered.

Part Three

Chapter Eleven

As a baby, Red Fur could not control her trunk. When she drank, half the water spilled to the ground. When she wrapped her nose around a clump of grass, she could not squeeze tightly enough and the grass slipped away. Frustrated, Red Fur reached out again. The long summer grass giggled and slipped away. One dry stalk poked Red Fur in the eye. Bits of crushed grass tickled the tip of her trunk. Sneezing, she backed into the branches of a juniper tree.

Red Fur's older sister came to stand beside the calf. The adolescent rumbled reassuringly and, looking for a distraction, led Red Fur to a heap of dung recently deposited by the matriarch. Eagerly Red Fur folded her knobby knees on the ground and ate the sticky stuff, her face and chin smeared, her trunk in the way so that she jerked it hard—as if to get rid of the thing altogether. Nearby Half Ear let out a sound of amusement. The bacteria in her dung would grow in Red Fur's stomach and help her child digest the bark of trees and brush. Yawning, the matriarch grazed lightly and napped for a few minutes, tired from the herd's most recent walk.

Soon Half Ear was dreaming about her own childhood,

filled with sweeter and better grass. Old Man was kinder then. Old Woman was more beautiful. Suddenly one of her daughters bumped her hard. Irritated, the matriarch stood straight, leaned back, and pushed the other mammoth away. The daughter rumbled and Half Ear opened her eyes, fully alert, turning and flapping her ears. Red Fur was nowhere in sight.

Curling up her trunk, the matriarch called as the rest of the herd stood quietly, listening for a reply. Wheeling, Half Ear ran toward a clump of trees in the distance, crashing through them as though they were stalks of grass. The trunks of the young ash snapped and splintered while branches tangled in the matriarch's fur and dragged behind her. The other mammoths followed, screaming, trumpeting, trampling the little forest that had grown up beside a new spring.

A yellow lion sat crouched and balanced on Red Fur's back, trying to claw through the coat and skin. His teeth had already raked the calf's shoulder and the lion could still taste that blood, which is why he had not heard the cries of the family or why he had heard but not been able to leave his prey. This was an older hungry male, harried from his pride when a stranger tore the flesh from his leg while all the lionesses simply watched. The outcast lion had not eaten in days. A lost baby mammoth looked too tempting.

At first Red Fur had been so startled by the weight on her back that she caught her breath and held it. But when she heard her mother's call, she began to squeal piteously, and she was squealing now as the entire herd rushed to the scene, snapping trees on every side.

Too late, the lion disengaged his claws and jumped from the baby's slippery shoulder. The matriarch slapped him with her trunk, a terrible blow to his wounded leg. Desperately the lion showed his teeth and caught the matriarch's ear, tearing off half before the mammoth used her foot to kick him unconscious. Another mammoth stepped on him and another began to fling the carcass to the ground, over and over.

"That's why we call you Half Ear," I said to the necklace, who was telling me this story.

The matriarch did not like to be interrupted. After a pause, her whispery voice continued in the darkness. This was an important moment for Red Fur, an early lesson in pain and blood. Some mammoths might have become timid, fearful of other animals, afraid to venture away from their family group. But not Red Fur, Half Ear said proudly. Soon her daughter was back chasing the horses and camels who grazed too close to the mammoth herd. Clumsy, determined, the baby mammoth galloped across the plain, the claw marks on her shoulder not yet healed, her trunk loose, her little tail high. She would return thirsty and drink from her mother, a long suckling that satisfied them both.

Half Ear liked to tell me about Red Fur, so that I felt I had raised this calf myself, watching it grow, measuring its progress. Red Fur fulfilled her early promise. Carefully she watched the other females and in her first estrus attracted a big bull, with whom she conceived. Two years later, she became a mother. Eventually she was the mother of many mammoths, quick to defend the herd, a faithful midwife, a tireless walker, a good judge of grass, a good judge of soil. The matriarch had died happy, knowing Red Fur would become the new matriarch. She had watched her daughter walk away, not needing to be told and not able to say good-bye. Paralyzed, her heart leaking, Half Ear rumbled for Chi to kill her. Gratefully she had waited for him.

Over the years the mammoth necklace told me many stories about her children and grandchildren, Big Penis and Little Penis, Big Ivory and Little Ivory, so many births and deaths that they became mixed up not only with each other but with my stories as well, my births and deaths. Now I am older than anyone I know, except for Crane, and the two families live together in my mind, Half Ear, Red Fur, Sage, Ali, Chi, Fat Bull, Five Legs, Second Crow. Their lives blur, as do my memories, skipping like stones over water.

Of course some deaths will always stand out, landmarks on the horizon, tethering my journey. It seems I am always traveling there.

I remember burying Bram. Next to me, Sage cried, tears for a man who could no longer chew his own meat, whose hands twisted like the joints of a cactus and whose teeth hurt so badly he whimpered with pain. We left Bram with three of his best points. We all felt sad, for he was the last of our elders, my uncle's generation.

Sage was much younger than her husband. She was strong and healthy, our storyteller, and still she decided to die too, forgetting to eat and careless about her safety. Even now I find it hard to forgive my sister.

We covered Etol with red ochre. It seemed to me then, and perhaps to others, that I should be more like Sage, Bram's wife. My grief should be fatal. Like my father, Etol had been hunting horses when he was surprised and struck by the stallion of the herd. This time the stallion's hoof landed high, denting Etol's forehead so that he fell without a sound. A day later he stopped breathing. As with Crow, I saw those strange holes in the air, that absence in camp where my husband should have been. Sometimes I saw a rippling movement as though someone had just left that space. Sometimes in the night I felt his body next to mine, a gentle roll against my thigh.

Again I survived the loss.

My two brothers died together. Wolf and Vole were on the plain, looking for mammoths and hunting with Etol's two sons. They did not find any mammoths, of course, not even any tracks or dried dung. Instead they were caught in a stampede, mostly of buffalo but with other herds as well panicked by a great fire in the distance. This fire was set by a family on the edge of our hunting grounds. We did not blame them, for we often set fires ourselves.

One afternoon, my cousin Golden never woke from a nap in his tent, just like his mother, my old aunt.

The next winter, Wolf's wife suffered from diarrhea and Crane could not help her, although Crane was a good healer.

A snake bit Golden's wife so that her leg swelled twice its size and turned black. Soon she went blind and coughed to death.

Perhaps you are surprised that I grieve for Golden's wife. Her name was Reed, like my name, for the willow that grows near the lake where she was born. Surely you have heard of Willow and Reed and their friendship? I think that is a story still told in this camp.

At first Sage and I were afraid of Reed. We watched her carefully and judged her mistakes. When she was not there, we made fun of her speech, which sounded harsh to us, a sputtering of saliva between the gaps in her teeth. Her manner seemed abrupt and bold, and we wondered about a woman who could leave so easily her family group. Later I realized that we felt toward Reed the anger we did not feel toward Ali, a woman who had also left her group. Reed was the same age as Ali, and we watched especially how she treated Golden, her older husband. We feared she might attract one of the younger men in camp, perhaps Etol's sons, still waiting for those girls to turn into wives. My sister and I had a good time imagining all the ways this small lake woman, with a baby in her arms, could harm us.

Reed understood our fears better than we did. Her people more often took in strangers and she had watched them critically as we watched her. She knew she had to stay close to Golden, to lower her eyes and bend her head. She did not do this very well. As Sage and I suspected, Reed did not like to stay quietly in the background. Still for a long time she behaved just as we wanted her to behave, like a buffalo calf. She was a good mother and a faithful wife and every day she did her share of the work, so that Sage and I had nothing to talk about.

After her baby died of fever, Reed had no more children. Her two girls grew up fast, like Ali's twins, and soon they were running through camp, playing their games, learning how to hunt and gather and work stone in the way we do these things. Reed did not have any special skill and her abruptness continued to startle people. But she had the words to make us laugh. She was a fair mimic and said funny, insulting things to people with whom she had become friendly. These were good-humored jokes about Golden or Wolf or Wolf's wife, never about Crane or Vole or Sage.

When we crushed red ochre over Sage's body, Reed stayed near me, crying softly. I remembered then how she had sat by my sister telling stories in the lodge, always ready to pass her a gourd of water or bite of food. After Etol died, Reed helped me with small tasks like scraping hides and shelling nuts. She spent more time with me than my own daughter Ali, who never seemed to rest from her work. In those winters we still lived in the foxes' cave. To please Crane, we also built every year an outside tent for Ali and her family, myself, and Chi. This tent was colder and less comfortable than the lodge. Yet Golden and his wife asked to join us there. Reed often put her furs next to me, with Chi on the other side.

I knew that Reed needed me. She needed someone in this group to speak for her. When she started telling stories at night, I was surprised but I did not object. At first Reed only told stories from the lake people, which we thought were very entertaining.

Then one night she began the journey of Tewa and Tono, not her people's version but our own, the people of the crooked fang, ending in this valley with Tewa's descendants right here. Although I did not stop her, I felt awkward. It was strange hearing our story from Reed, and her dialect made it sound stranger, her emphasis wrong on certain words. At the same time I was impressed, for she knew the entire journey as Sage had known it, with the same gestures and silences.

When Crane heard about this the next day, she immediately complained. This woman, who drove us each winter into a tent, always worried about what we did there.

"Reed should not talk about Tewa and Tono," Crane said to Dipper's daughter as they worked on a hide.

"The children of Reed are the descendants of Tewa and Tono," I spoke out, "just like the children of Crane."

One night and one story would not have mattered. But Reed continued to tell stories until we saw what she wanted. She wanted to be an important person in our camp, what Sage had been, the woman in the lodge. This quarrel lasted a long time. In the end, Reed won because I was her ally—and more, for she became my friend in a way only Dipper had been when we were children. Perhaps it was like this for Tireus and Ali. I hope so.

I loved being with Reed. As we gathered seeds or wove willow, we laughed over jokes that lasted for days and even years, jokes about our jokes that made me cackle in a high voice. Sometimes we were so loud the other people in camp became disgusted. Usually that made me laugh harder. More than once, Crane told me to act my age. Then Reed would stand behind her, solemn as an owl, blinking this way and that, turning her head in a half circle. My people make fun of owls because these birds look so serious. Now Reed was making fun of Crane, only Crane could not see her. Crane and I were elders, like my old aunt. But no one had ever stood behind my aunt blinking stupidly, ruffling imaginary feathers, and whooing soundlessly with pursed lips. When Reed did this, I laughed so hard I urinated.

In the winter and summer, as we worked together, Reed and I told each other the stories of our lives. In this way they seemed new. I saw my people as a stranger might see them. I saw my life as a journey across a dangerous land, choosing different trails, never able to go back and choose again but always moving forward, stopping briefly at a place where the trail divides.

Of course, I was more interested in hearing about Reed, whose journey had been so much more dramatic.

"If you had spent a day with my co-wife," Reed explained, "you also would have left your family group. I was Golden's first wife. I had three children. Yet I had to tan her furs. I had to rub her feet. She had a voice . . . I cannot describe it. She spoke to us as though we were turtles."

Among the lake people, Reed's co-wife was powerful because she belonged to that group of men and women with canes in their noses. Reed did not speak about these people often, and she did not joke about them.

"They meet on the secret island," she said, "where they eat a plant that shows the future. Sometimes your daughter's husband goes with them. Sometimes he is not allowed to go. We have had the secret island longer than the shaman. When he dies, the bear spirit will leave us. But the island will always be there."

"What did they see, on that island?" I asked.

Reed shrugged. "They never told us."

She spoke with more humor about the shaman. Before the dark days, when he began to hurt people, this man was ridiculed by the younger women. They giggled about the lusty nature of the bear, who had been known to visit wives when their husbands were hunting.

"I saw the bear today," someone might confide to her friends.

"Was he fierce?" a woman would ask.

"Did he growl?" a woman would murmur.

"Was he big?" a woman would shriek.

All the women laughed and whispered, never talking about the thing directly but joking more wildly until the children came running to see the excitement. Sometimes a woman wondered if she was carrying a bear child. Sometimes a woman rejected the bear's visit, and then the shaman left her without a word, his handsome face sad. The women mocked that sad face too.

"Did you disappoint the bear?"

"Oh, poor bear!"

"Oh, sad bear!"

I teased Reed. "Did *you* disappoint the bear?"

"Yes," she said quickly. "The shaman was my cousin. Also I had Golden, a second wife, and babies in my tent. The bear could never find me alone."

Reed was clever in this way. She wanted me to know that all her children were from my people's lineage. When Golden asked her to leave her family, she had agreed, but she had also been afraid. Reed always thought ahead. She wondered how she would grow old in a new group. She knew that Golden might die first. Her son would leave to marry elsewhere. Only her daughters would remain to tie her here. Reed worried about this every day, until she decided to become our storyteller.

"I practiced all the time," she told me. "I went over Sage's words as I gathered, as I cooked, as I slept. I knew I would have to amaze you. I was afraid that Dipper's daughter was also learning the stories. I was afraid you were learning them."

"That was never my skill," I said lightly.

Years later, after Vole and Wolf and Golden were gone, Reed became one of our leaders, someone like my uncle who we turned to when we had to make a decision. I did not become a leader because I did not want to, and Crane did not because I would not let her. Instead it was Reed who sat at night before the central fire with Dipper's daughter and the daughter's husband and Etol's sons. It was Reed who discussed with them the movement of game or the best place for the spring gathering. They talked often about water and wells, and we changed camp nearly every month, up and down the dead river as Old Man burned stubbornly in the sky and the drought stretched into the days when my grandchildren had children of their own.

Reed was a leader when she died, bit by a snake, its tail shaking like seeds in a gourd. She joked about that, for she had always feared the big-headed water snakes in the lake where she was born.

"I could have stayed home," she said, "for this kind of death."

By now my friend had stopped spending time with me. Her needs were different and our jokes were not the same. I understood, although the taste was bitter when I saw her at the fire talking with Dipper's daughter.

In her last days I visited her tent and we held hands. My own hands hurt badly now, and my shoulders, and I had lost most of my teeth. I could not see directly ahead of me. Slowly that dark fuzzy patch would grow bigger, another hole in the world. Long ago I had stopped hunting and learned to depend on my relatives.

"I hope you win this contest," Reed teased me in a weak voice, just before she died. "I hope you live longer than Crane."

Alone at night I listened to the whispers of the mammoth necklace. The matriarch knew how I felt about Reed. She had also joked with her daughter Red Fur as they became more than mother and daughter, grazing together, sharing the dream of the grass in their stomachs. Half Ear enjoyed playing tricks on Red Fur, and Red Fur learned to tease back, smacking her mother's leg as easily as she would smack an adolescent.

One day Half Ear and Red Fur stumbled into the territory of a nesting bird trying to hatch her eggs. The little brown bird flew out of the grass to flap its wings at the big mammoths. Half Ear was sensitive to the dignity of another mother. Delicately she backed away, bumping into Red Fur grazing behind her. Red Fur had not seen the bird, and she grumbled loudly. The bird flew up again, pretending now to have a broken wing. The mammoths were so huge they were all the mother bird could see—and still she flapped her wings at these mountains, leading them away from her eggs.

Half Ear kept backing up, pushing against her daughter and making the sound of amusement. Red Fur swerved to avoid the matriarch's tail in her face. Then Red Fur saw the fluttering bird and understood. She also made the sound of amusement. Even so, again Half Ear backed up, chasing her daughter in that backward funny way until Red Fur saw that this was a game. Trumpeting, she wrapped her trunk around Half Ear's tail and jerked it hard. The mother bird gave a fierce cry, flying up once more before returning to her nest, her head cocked, her eyes bright with triumph.

Half Ear and Red Fur laughed and laughed.

Chapter Twelve

I know what you are thinking. You say I have forgotten Ali. You insist quietly, "What happened to your daughter?"

Ali was surely Tewa's granddaughter although she did not bear as many children. Still, she filled my old age with babies, as she filled our camp. She gave up all her blood.

I never liked Ali's second husband. Sage said I was behaving badly but I said my daughter did not need another man so soon after she returned to her family group. Ali came to us in late summer and mated with my new son-in-law at the next spring gathering. For marriage gifts, she used what she had brought with her from the south, things she could carry easily, plants to make a woman barren, herbs for a fever, red root for stomach pain. The mother of this boy was a healer, and she valued these gifts so much she happily gave up her only son. The man himself burned under the eye of Old Woman. Eager to join us, he seemed to me a shadow man, anxiously following the leaders of our camp, following my daughter like a camp dog. When I said this out loud, Sage only smiled and shook her head.

At least his penis worked. By that summer my daughter was already pregnant. In the spring she had a healthy girl. Three springs later, she had another girl. When that child was weaned, she had a boy. When that boy was weaned, she had another!

By this time, her twins, the children of the shaman, were old enough to marry as well. I was surprised when my daughter wanted me to find them husbands.

"Watch at the circle," she asked.

"Talk to the family," she begged.

"These are good choices," she reassured me when I pointed out two strong healthy men. "Before I saw the bear, this is what I wanted for myself."

Even as one twin carried her second son, Ali felt her own stomach swell again. Reed could not help but make jokes. What was the secret of the sharp-toothed mountain? Its women were as fertile as red spiders. I grinned as Reed poked fun at every animal who births easily, from the beetle to the lioness. Secretly I was proud. The shaman had thrown two of my grandchildren into the water of the lake. But here Ali bloomed like a plum tree—and all her babies lived. Her strong hands protected them. Her breasts filled with milk. I was frankly in awe of my daughter.

When Ali had her last child, she was as old as I was the day I became a completed woman. The children of my grandchildren could already speak, yet my daughter walked through camp wearing a skin cape that barely covered her. She seemed bigger than usual, and people gossiped that she would have twins.

This seemed lucky to us, and we needed luck. A month before, early that fall, the buffalo stampeded and their frantic bodies dragged my brothers to the ground. The sharp hooves cut Wolf in half. They splintered Vole's bones. Now the camp was dismal. Wolf's wife looked thin—and Crane too. In a short time, we would be moving to the winter lodge, away from this sadness.

I remember Chi surrounded by a group of young boys, mostly his nephews, Ali's son and Wolf's grandsons. Chi worked slowly on a fluted point, making sure that the boys understood each step. He tapped a long flake from the base of a stone so that the point would sit firmly in the spear. When the stone broke, the children groaned. Chi shrugged and put the broken pieces aside to shape later into smaller points.

"We'll start again," he said. He was not a very good stone worker. Flint, especially, did not care for him. But he was, sometimes, a good teacher. Still unmarried, our bachelor bull, he spent much of his time alone and even hunted alone in the pink canyons, although he knew this made me nervous.

At Crane's tent, I left a bag of pine nuts. With my brothers dead, I had new obligations toward their wives. Both women had left their family group, and they would be very sensitive now. Fortunately they had girls to tie them to this camp.

Most of the young people were at the river, digging a new well. At the central fire, Wolf's wife and her daughters sat cooking together, something made of vole and mice, small things we ate more often as the grazing animals suffered and died. The herds on the plain ranged widely, moving constantly from grass to grass. Hunting was harder and more dangerous. Other predators watched us closely and tried to take our meat. We lost frequently to lions and packs of wolves. Always the vultures, condors, and teratorns circled above our heads, their dark wings blocking the sun. Sometimes we saw new animals from the north coming over the mountains behind us, following the streams drying to dust. The saber-toothed cats traveled alone, hunted by lions who tore them apart whenever they could. Desperate for food, one saber-toothed cat even entered our camp and killed a small boy from Dipper's lineage. Giant short-faced bears still hibernated in the forest and if we found one of these, we dug it out and killed it with our spears. Whenever I ate that meat, I thought of Crow.

From Crane's tent, I passed Chi again and stopped to watch him work. Triumphant, my son held up a good chert point, bloodred in the afternoon light.

"Shall I get you a deer today?" he asked.

"Can I come?" a boy quickly begged.

"No!" Chi gave him a friendly push.

"I'll make you a shirt," I promised my son. There were more pine nuts to gather but I could leave those for Reed and the other women. I was pleased to do something for Chi.

"Let me look at Ali now," I said happily.

My daughter lay in half darkness with the flap to her tent closed. Her youngest boy napped beside her, one small hand curled around his genitals. This made me smile. I had seen my son sleep like this and Etol too.

"I think the baby will come soon," Ali whispered, trying not to wake the child.

That changed my plans. "Will you stay in here," I asked, "or go outside?" Many women prefer to birth outside where the liquids and blood can soak easily into the ground. The afterbirth is gathered and buried far away.

"In here," Ali said, "but I need more moss."

My daughter's labors were always quick. She hardly needed me or Reed or Wolf's wife, although we still came to be with her in the tent, eating pine nuts and mush from the seeds of summer. Soon Ali stumbled outside to let her waters break. She was not quick enough and came back with soaked leggings. I could hear Chi laughing.

"What will you do with all these children?" he yelled. "I think you will be busy."

"Where is your husband?" Wolf's wife wondered.

"I don't know," Ali grunted.

"I saw him with Golden," Reed put in.

"Tonight he can sleep by the central fire," I said.

"His sons are with the twins," Wolf's wife murmured.

I did not know which twins she meant, hers or Ali's, and I simply nodded. We were only chatting, passing the time. At births like these, with these women, I missed my sister, Sage, the most. She belonged here in this circle. Again I felt angry with her.

Ali squatted and clenched her teeth. As the darkness and cold deepened, Reed built a fire under the smoke hole and prepared bundles of pine pitch in case we needed light. Over the fire, she sprinkled leaves of honey bush. Wolf's wife laid out antelope strips.

Ali kept moving, squatting, hiding her face in her arms. The contractions rippled the tight skin of her stomach, and she groaned impatiently. I reached for another handful of pine nuts. Her pain made me anxious. Her body looked exhausted, the lips of her vagina hanging down, the skin on her legs rough and wrinkled and patterned with scars. Her black hair had already turned gray. Her feet were splayed with the weight of babies. In the flickering light, I mourned the youth of my first daughter, a grandmother herself, gritting her teeth, groaning and bursting.

"This labor," I said at last, "is taking too long."

Then Reed went to get Crane, who brought with her the daughter of her daughter.

"She has small hands," Crane explained.

Ali lay on her back, grimacing while the healer ungently felt her stomach. Suddenly Crane pushed hard, trying to move the baby's head. When Ali cried out, Crane looked puzzled. She pushed again, although I could see she did not know where the child was.

Now the girl put her hand into my daughter to turn the baby so it would face the earth, ready to be born. Ali whimpered and the girl whimpered too as the contractions squeezed her fingers and wrist. In a scolding voice, Crane told her what to do.

"Can you feel the buttocks?" she asked. "Push them here."

"No, I can't move them," the girl gasped. When she pulled out her hand, her knuckles were black.

Crane and I stared at each other.

Jerking upward, Ali shrieked without restraint! A blue claw came out of her body. The tiny hand seemed to beckon and grab the air. The arching of Ali's stomach caused another contraction which drew in the baby's arm, in and out, in and out. As small as an acorn, the hand spasmed and waved its fingers. It seemed to be reaching for life outside the womb. Ali rocked in agony. As though from a distance, faintly, I heard Crane sigh. There would be no life tonight. This child was already dead. Slowly and painfully, Ali would die too.

Some stories say this is what happened to our grandmother Tewa, that she died an old woman past childbearing with a last baby trapped in her womb. In these stories, Tewa never screamed as waves of birth wedged more tightly the stillborn daughter against her pelvis. Lying beside her husband in their tent, Tewa only waited patiently. When she closed her eyes, Tono closed his, and the three of them were buried together to talk under the earth about the future of this land.

When we buried Ali, I could still hear her screams, raw living things, my daughter screaming. Crane gave her willow bark for the pain, but nothing could ever stop that pain, for it was also rage and despair. We all felt it.

"She had grandchildren," Crane reminded me at the burial. "She had a long life."

At the very end I held my daughter while her husband and children wept nearby, inside the tent and outside the tent, all around camp. Ali was bleeding from her nose and mouth, her vagina and ears, from the holes in her skin. Her blood seeped into the pads of moss the other women had gathered. I remember the cold early light of morning. My daughter breathed weakly, fluttering sounds like a bird in a snare. My body felt like hers, swollen with tears, a dead child in my stomach.

After that, I aged quickly. We buried Golden, we buried Wolf's wife, we buried Reed. The dark spot grew in front of my eyes. I lost so many teeth that the son of my grandson had to chew my food, placing gobs of meat respectfully on my thigh. I walked so slowly that sometimes Chi carried me on his back to the spring gathering. Other times, the people left me in camp with a sullen grandchild. I was a burden, yet I was not a burden, for my family boasted about me and Crane to groups who did not have elders so old. It took wealth to support the two of us.

By then I knew my special skill. It was not hunting mammoths like my uncle or bearing children like my daughter. My skill was living, while all the others died.

Chapter Thirteen

For many years, I sat by the fire and told stories. After Reed was bitten by a snake, I tried to tell Sage's stories but I was never good at this, worse even than my old aunt. Finally Dipper's daughter took over the job. I was better at entertaining children with Dog and White Bear and tales of stalking mammoths. I told them about my first hunt among the pink rocks of the narrow canyon. Etol killed the baby with his spear. The child died instantly and we feasted that night on meat so tender it fell apart in our mouths, hot chunks of mammoth meat sparkling with fat. I have often thought of that meal, so rich and flavorful.

I told the children about walking across the yellow plain, past little forests of juniper and oak, my spear balanced, my shoulder blades prickling into wings. As though this were the story of Tono and his son Hau, a journey of men with legs like tree roots, I talked about myself and what I had been. Once I traveled for days to reach the camp of Dipper's husband's people. The hills rose up in new shapes and I wanted to keep walking all the way to the salty water that spreads everywhere. If it had not been for Chi, I might have kept traveling—as far as Tono—for I was that strong, casting my net over the land. I remembered all this as though it had happened to someone else.

I told the children about Red Fur and Half Ear.

"She was taller than your father's winter tent," I said to the son of my youngest granddaughter, "and as wide as five men standing beside each other. She came through the summer grass and stepped on the heart of my first husband."

"Then Chi killed her!" a girl exclaimed.

"Much later," I said. "Years later when your great-uncle was a man. He made a necklace of her ivory and that necklace is wrapped in deerskin in my tent."

"How can an animal as big as a tent have a nose that

reaches down to the ground?" a boy wondered. Some of the children laughed.

"It is like a tapir," I said. "Think of its long nose."

"We have never seen a tapir," my great-grandson reminded me.

"It is like the giant insect-eater," I tried.

"I have never seen the giant insect-eater," a girl said. "That is a story like White Bear and Dog."

I was tired of talking to these children. "Do you think you cannot believe in animals?" I asked them.

"We know there are mammoths," my great-grandson tried to please me, "because we have ivory. We have their tusks."

"My father has never seen a mammoth," the girl still argued.

"I have seen them." I spoke sharply. "Uncle Chi has seen them and other people in this camp."

Now the girl did not reply and I leaned over to peer, half blind, into her face. Who did she belong to? She behaved like a member of Crane's family.

"What else do you not believe in?" I tried to tease the child. She only stared at the ground.

I thought of the last time I had seen mammoths.

Ali and Chi were recently returned to our camp. Sage was alive and I hunted again with Etol and Golden. On this day, one of Crane's daughters—the youngest and boldest—also came with us. We looked for camels because Sage wanted to dance the camel ceremony for Golden's children. For this, she needed fresh hides and feet as part of her costume. Etol saw the mammoth tracks first and we followed them for the excitement of watching a bachelor herd. We could smell their musk a long distance away, sharp, sour, rank. The men

touched their genitals for luck. Crane's daughter and I glanced at each other, trying not to smile. Men love to watch male mammoths, especially when females are nearby. The more serious the men acted, the more this girl and I wanted to laugh.

Of course, a mammoth in rut is extremely dangerous. Suddenly he might charge at a bush or decide to stomp some animal to death. He is moody and unpredictable, angry at a mouse in the grass or a lion on the hill. A bachelor herd is smelly, noisy, and terrifying. For this reason, the hunters in my family sought them out whenever they could and talked about them proudly at the central fire. The other men were always envious.

"Was Big Penis there?" someone would ask.

"Did you see White Ear?" another would wonder.

As we neared this herd, we climbed a small hill and screened ourselves carefully in the scrub brush. Our own scent was lost in the dust kicked up by the nervous mammoths and in their sprays of urine. The gaunt, loose-skinned males hardly grazed on the brittle summer grass but spent their time watching each other, avoiding the bulls who were in full rut. Those mammoths spurted a slimy liquid down their hindquarters and whipped their long penises back and forth. Gallumphing on five legs, they snorted, trumpeted, and occasionally tried to mate with a smaller bull.

I heard the knocking of tusks before I saw the two animals locked in combat, pressing their ivories together, falling apart, rushing each other, slamming their tusks again. They fought in a large meadow surrounded by pine trees. The animals looked well matched, which is why they had come to blows. They might fight like this for hours until one of them retreated or died. The rest of the herd moved away, scattering discreetly into the forest. I wanted to move away too, for the angry bulls were uncomfortably close. The thunk of their tusks frightened me.

"I choose White Ear," Etol whispered to Golden.

"He is already wounded," Golden said low.

"No!" I protested. I have known men to stay in the bushes and watch most of the day as two males fought. Once my uncle built a fire and waited all night to see the outcome of a battle. That is how my father lost a good bone shaft wrench, betting with his brother.

"No." Crane's daughter also spoke firmly.

"We are looking for camels," I reminded Golden.

My cousin paused and then nodded. He was an amiable man. But Etol, who loved to gamble, glared at me. I would hear more about this in our tent.

"A few minutes longer," my husband muttered.

As I waited, I did not hide my feelings. The rank smell in those bushes made me wrinkle my nose.

That evening when we described the bulls before the central fire, Sage also looked annoyed. We had come home without any camel feet but only a peccary and two rabbits in Etol's pack. My sister began to scold a young boy playing near the drying racks. We knew she was really scolding Golden and Etol.

Later, however, I would regret not staying to watch the bachelor herd. That was the last any of us saw a living mammoth. The males soon left our area, searching for females in estrus, and their semen fell uselessly on the ground. I saw the dried puddles when we returned to the place where we had hidden in the scrub brush. There we found the body of the mammoth called White Ear, the gaping wound in his neck black with flies. Etol and I did not need ivory, so we let Golden give the tusks to Reed, who shaped them into marriage gifts for her daughters.

Since then, the daughters of those daughters have had daughters.

I frowned at the children in a circle around me. They were quiet. "Who is your mother?" I asked the girl who stared at the ground. It bothered me that so many men in our family had never hunted mammoths. What would happen when Red Fur came back? Who would teach these hunters?

That night I unwrapped my bundle of deerskin and wore the necklace against my chest. I also kept certain plants in this bundle and the blue stones given to me when I married Etol. Chi slept nearby, in my tent. Briefly he glanced at the ivory beads before turning on his side. I do not think he ever heard the matriarch as she whispered in the dark, although sometimes his snoring disturbed *us*.

I told the matriarch a story that had been in my mind all day. I remembered this story when the girl who stared at the ground gave me her mother's name, the daughter of Wolf's stepdaughter.

When Ali's twins were newly married, the largest twin was bitten by a badger. The animal became angry because the girls, gathering berries, blocked him from the entrance to his home. Uneasily the badger waited for these bad-smelling strangers to move. He snuffled a warning. But the twins were talking and did not hear. Finally, after one human leg nearly brushed his nose, the badger lunged, ripped open flesh, and hurried into his hole.

Crane came to the tent where Ali worked with poultices of herbs. My granddaughter's leg swelled, she grew feverish, and infection ran like red ants up her thigh. To our surprise, Reed came forward now and explained what the people of the lake would do. Reed wanted us to ask the badger to withdraw his poison. She said we needed to leave him gifts, not at the entrance to his home, but deep inside where he slept during the day. Most of us thought this would be a dangerous and useless task. None of us wanted to crawl into a badger's hole! Crane scoffed but Reed looked at Ali, and Ali nodded. She had seen stranger healings by the people of the lake.

Now Reed said that whoever went into the badger's home

had to be a woman unrelated to the injured girl. Reed could not go because she was the shaman's cousin. All the other women in our camp were also related to Ali and her children, except for Wolf's wife and his two stepdaughters. The new husband of my granddaughter began to argue with Reed—he wanted to go himself—but she was firm. At last he sat on the ground and covered his eyes.

After some discussion, the woman whose mother had died of bad teeth agreed to help us. At the badger's hole, we dug out some of the entrance so this woman could squeeze her way in. I could hear, inside, the animal stirring. Wolf's stepdaughter was afraid, but she was also brave, and she put our gifts in front of her face as a kind of protection. Wrinkling her nose, she wormed into the musty den. In a few seconds, we saw her rear end wiggling back out.

When we returned to camp, my granddaughter was sleeping peacefully! She would never even limp on that leg. From then on I took more notice of Wolf's stepdaughter. I praised her at the central fire and gave her an antelope skin for her marriage to a boy from the north.

I told the matriarch this story, about healing and about gifts, to show her that my people could be generous. Wolf's stepdaughter had been generous. I had been generous.

The necklace liked my story and gave me one of her own.

Once she adopted a calf whose mother had died. Half Ear had recently given birth, so she had milk in her teats that two youngsters could share. Unfortunately the adopted male had to steal this milk whenever he could, for his new sibling was aggressively jealous. Determined, the little male endured his sister's attacks until she gave in and let him nurse. The matriarch watched all this with interest, happy to see that the male would live.

One day, at the beginning of the drought, Half Ear led her herd to some mineral deposits she had not visited in many years. Using their tusks, the mammoths lifted the white dust and inhaled its salty flavor. The matriarch rumbled approvingly. Next she took her daughters and sons, granddaughters and grandsons, to a pond some distance away. Other animals on the plain were also moving toward this pond, and the matriarch hurried as she felt the vibrations of buffalo, camels, and horses running behind her, growing in number as more animals met and joined the herd. The matriarch lifted her trunk to sniff for smoke. If this was a fire, it was not close. Still she sensed an urgency in the air.

At the water, Half Ear was surprised to see large areas of the pond had turned into thick treacherous muck. Pushing with her heavy shoulders she tried to keep her family away from the tempting mud. She wanted them to drink quickly and leave before the buffalo came. But even as she rumbled, the adopted male wandered off and became stuck. When he squealed, two adolescent females rushed to help him. Now they were also trapped in the black goo! Their cries excited the rest of the family and some of the younger males began sparring with each other, butting their heads in confusion.

The front wave of buffalo, mixed with other animals, approached the pond in a brown cloud. The adopted male, his white ear flapping, sank into the sticky mud. The matriarch trumpeted, a signal to the older females, who lined up in a row confronting the galloping animals. Even these massive bison paused at the sight of so many mammoths.

Like water parts around a rock, the buffalo streamed around the big females.

Meanwhile the matriarch and Red Fur waded into the pond to free the trapped male and frightened adolescents. First one young mammoth broke from the suction and then the other. Red Fur held the baby's head so he could breathe while Half Ear pushed her tusks deep into the mud, struggling to keep her balance. With a bellow, she heaved up. The male lifted slightly into the air. Red Fur caught him with her trunk and threw him sideways. Deftly she pushed him again, sliding him over the mud until his feet touched land and he staggered upright.

Rumbling, Half Ear and Red Fur now joined the line of females. They stayed there trembling until all the buffaloes had reached the pond and settled around its edges. The baby calf also trembled and the matriarch nuzzled him, touching his glands. He was doubly blessed, she said, to be rescued twice in his short life.

"He grew very big," the necklace finished, "and went to live with the bachelor bulls. One day he caught his sister and mated with her. Their calf was a healthy female. She also grew up to mate with a bull."

The matriarch began the list of her children, a long line of descendants that gave her much pleasure to recite. This was another story of family, survival, and gifts. This story should have comforted me.

But I was not comforted. My stomach was hollow like a cave full of spirits. I felt uneasy. The matriarch had lifted her trunk to smell smoke. She had sensed a fire, an urgency. But there was no fire. Why were the animals running across the plain?

I sensed something terrible. I could not name what it was. I thought of the bachelor herd, looking for females. I thought of a dream I had had long ago, of those absences in camp when Crow and Etol died, how the still air rippled. Now the land itself seemed to ripple, shimmering with emptiness. These children had never seen a tapir. They had never seen a mammoth.

"When will Red Fur return?" I asked the necklace. I had asked this many times before.

"I see Red Fur walking," the matriarch said, "taking the herd to new water holes."

"When will she return?" I asked again.

"People wait by the water," the necklace spoke, "and kill the granddaughters who are already weak."

"But Red Fur escapes?"

The necklace was silent.

Now something quite amazing happened. I was most amazed because the matriarch was also amazed, alarmed, and thrilled.

I was traveling with the matriarch and Red Fur. We walked through the bristly summer grass in Red Fur's body, brushing aside catclaw with our heavy wrinkled legs. We were deeply tired, deeply depressed. Looking out, I saw a series of hills rising from a land covered dully in scrub brush. The sky shimmered white. I was seeing colors only mammoths see. I could hear the complaints of other mammoths behind me and the glands near my ears began to leak with sorrow and anticipation, for I smelled water and I knew that water was dangerous. I tested the air with the tip of my trunk. I tried to stop myself from running but I was too thirsty. The heat in my body became a reckless longing. My tail lifted. My ears flapped.

Oh, the scent of the pond filled me with happiness. As the cool water swelled my nose, I squirted liquid into my mouth, over and over, greedy for more. The rest of the herd pushed against my thighs as we all drank and jostled for room. Mud and water splashed my dry coat. My skin itched to be clean but I did not lie down or roll in the pond. We had to hurry.

"Hurry!" I rumbled as I squirted and slurped. We could not stay here. "Hurry!"

Next to me, suddenly, the daughter of my sister screamed.

As I turned, I saw a long stick pierce her neck. Another stick shook in the tender gland behind her eye. Her children and other relatives also screamed and began to panic, bumping against her and pushing the stick deeper into her flesh. She was an older female who had mated with a bull two years ago. We had been so grateful to see that bull! We joined with him vigorously, jubilantly, although only this niece and myself had conceived. Each of us now had a calf in our womb.

My sister's daughter staggered as more sticks hit her body and ripped through her shaggy coat. She tilted toward the water that opened for her. I saw the perfectly formed fetus slide out from beneath her dark leg. It was a female still wrapped in the torn placenta. The tiny baby floated toward me, buoyed by the bloody sac that enclosed her.

For a moment, the trumpets and cries of the ambushed mammoths quieted. I was Willow, Red Fur, and the necklace of the matriarch. We focused on that thin red line, the blood trailing the baby in the water.

"Run!" Red Fur screamed, and part of me galloped away with the herd, following Red Fur as she led the few of us who remained to safety.

Another part of me stayed behind and butchered the pregnant female, slicing through thick fur, dragging flesh and bones out of the pond, shouting as I saw the fetus. I knew there would be arguments about this prize. I recognized some of the people around me. This was the family of the boy who had married Dipper's daughter.

Willow stood crying on the bank.

I wept in my bed and the necklace of the matriarch burned cold. "Red Fur," I wept.

Then Red Fur came to me. She stood in my tent. She was so big that her shoulders touched the upper hides of camel and horse. Her head lifted and the poles that met at the smoke hole snapped and the animal hides tore at their seams and the tent broke apart, flying off into the night with its bright stars. I looked over at my son, who still slept on the ground undisturbed. I could see him clearly.

Red Fur smelled of wet hide, grass, and dung. Her scarred trunk was creased with wrinkles. Her tusks curved over my body as she rested them lightly on my legs. One tusk had broken in half. High, like the stars, her tiny eyes glittered. I looked into her womb and saw the movement of a male calf. Its trunk curled like an unopened fern. The fetus kicked, ready to be born.

Red Fur was here. Then she was gone.

All night I lay awake thinking. Finally I woke Chi and told him what had happened. He passed a hand over his face, trying to understand.

"Red Fur came here," he said, "and the tent flew apart?"

He gestured. The tent was standing.

"She came with a message," I whispered dramatically.

Chi shrugged. This was not his skill.

I went outside where the morning's pink light was just touching the tops of the pine trees. The spring day felt full of promise. As old as I was, I felt that promise too, a green sap rising in my veins. The heavy weight of my loneliness fell away.

Surely this dream had only one meaning.

Old Man loves us. Old Woman loves us.

Surely Red Fur and the herd would be coming back soon. The empty spaces of the plain would fill with the sounds of mammoths, camels, llamas, antelope, horses, and buffalo, shaking the ground as they swept across the land. The empty holes on the plain would fill with animals.

There are things in this world and in us that can never be lost.

With this, I went to the central fire.

Chapter Fourteen

The drought ended the next day. Perhaps I am wrong about this. Perhaps another spring passed or a summer or a fall. I remember only that after Red Fur came to my tent, I began to hear rain at night. That winter we had storms that turned the world white and new. When the days grew warm, the river ran with melted snow. White flowers bloomed on the long shanks of hills, yellow flowers by the streams and ponds. I could smell them from my place in camp and the children brought me petals to crush in my hands. I could smell grass and earth and, in the fall again, I smelled the leaves dying. I told Chi that soon he would be hunting mammoths.

"No, I'm too old for that." My son sat so close to me his breath hissed in my ear. More people did that as my hearing grew worse.

"The rains will bring them," I said happily.

"Maybe," Chi shouted.

"What does the husband of Dipper's daughter say?"

Chi did not respond. He did not get along well with the leaders in our camp. Oddly, Crane's family proved to be a better ally for him. I knew too that my daughter's children would always give their uncle food and shelter. I no longer worried about Chi.

"The granddaughter of Dipper's daughter is pregnant," Chi yelled suddenly.

"Good!" I said.

"No, Mother, because she has no husband. She mated with a cousin."

This was bad news. I hoped our healer could quickly kill the child in the womb.

"That happened to Sage." I surprised myself by saying this out loud. "She mated with a cousin at a spring gathering before she married her first husband. They killed the baby inside her. After that, she never had children."

Again Chi said nothing. I think he was also surprised.

"What are they doing with this girl and her cousin?" I wanted to hear more of the story.

"They are talking about it."

"Now? At the central fire?"

"Yes, at the fire," Chi said irritably. "This camp is crazy. I might go away for a while."

My son was right. The camp was crazy. That night no one thought to bring me meat or help me inside the tent where I slept with my granddaughter's family. So I stayed where I was, wrapped in furs, as the night air turned cold and I could hear around me, whispering like the matriarch's necklace, the deaths of many small insects.

Early that morning, the sky still dark and the light uncertain, I rose stiffly. I needed to defecate.

Even half blind, I could find my way to a path and clump of small-needled trees. When I finished burying my scat, I walked farther down the trail toward the river. I did not think about this clearly. I did not make a decision to die, as Chi later accused me of doing. I only wanted to see the river again. I wanted to smell the water and gather willow branches that I would tell a grandchild to weave into a basket.

I went toward that smell painfully. The swollen joints in my fingers hurt. My shoulders ached. My hips burned. My gums were sore, and I thought often of the woman with bad teeth, the woman who had screamed and moaned all summer. Fortunately I did not have the stabbing pain that means an abscess. Every morning I tested the remaining teeth in my mouth, anxiously touching their familiar edges. Walking now, I probed these teeth again with the tip of my tongue.

The darkness ahead of me seemed to grow larger. In the corners of sight, I saw yellowing leaves and vines turning brown. Winter was coming. Did we still move to a winter lodge? I couldn't remember. Stumbling, I almost fell and the pain in my hip made me angry. Unhappily I tried to move my fingers. I would not gather willow branches today.

The lion must have heard my noise and attacked from the side, pushing me to the ground, pinning me with his heavy paws. After the shock, my legs and chest went numb.

I waited like a young buffalo or horse, suddenly calm, for the teeth to rip out chunks of my flesh. I have seen this happen to other animals and I have always wondered what they felt.

I waited calmly for a long time before I realized that too much time was passing. From under my shoulder came the smell of something sweet and tangy, a crushed plant. There was no lion smell, no scent of blood or rotting food—only the faint memory of Jak and a brush of his essence. Grass tickled the back of my neck as I lay on the dewy earth, my head slanting awkwardly. There was no lion. I had fallen down a slope. I moaned in disgust.

Still I was afraid to move, to lose that numbness in my hip. At the same time, I did not want to stay here with my head facing the wrong way and my thighs open for anyone to see!

I moaned again, hoping that a real lion might hear me.

Then I stopped because I wanted to be buried properly, with red ochre on my face and arms, with my bones still whole.

Later in the day, some boys set out to snare rabbits and found my upturned feet instead. Dipper's husband came himself to carry me to camp. Crane's daughter sent a hunter after Chi, although no one thought he would be found in time.

I should have known not to fear lions. Long ago my father, Wolf, Etol, and I spoke sternly to a lioness and drove her from her meat. That lioness scarred my son but she did not kill him. Also, the skin animal of my first husband was a lion, and I lived with him for many years. We fought bitterly but he did not kill me. We had some kind of love for each other, even if I could not grieve his death.

No, it was the bear, the giant short-faced bear that came to the bed where I lay dying and raked me with her claws, roaring so that I shrieked with terror. My heart pounded as though it were a drum and the bear a shaman beating the drum. Always this giant bear has pursued me. First she took one daughter and then she took the other. Now she came to rip me apart and stuff me in her gaping mouth so that nothing would remain, not a scrap, not a sliver of bone. I felt her rage and power. I screamed and screamed.

"She is asleep."

I heard Crane's voice.

"What happened?"

Chi's breath hissed in my ear.

I opened my eyes. "The bear," I whispered.

"What happened?" Chi accused me.

I reached out for the face of my son. The bear was gone. This was only the helpless anger of a boy. Chi has always been angry with me. I should have given his father the mammoth tusk. I regretted that. I regretted dying before I could see the mammoth herd again. I regretted dying before Crane.

Chi took my hand and began to cry.

When I awoke again, he and Crane were still in the tent, arguing.

"The necklace should stay with the people," Crane said.

"The necklace belongs to her." Chi was fierce.

"She gave it to me once," Crane replied. "It is really mine."

At this, I tried to sit up. Crane had refused the necklace!

She had taken my best wolf parka!

Chapter Fifteen

 Now I am done with this story.

Now I wonder who you are.

At times I thought I was talking to one of my great-grandchildren, a boy sitting quietly, listening to an old woman dying. Perhaps, I thought, you will grow up to be one of our leaders, a man like my uncle who will remember the things I say here and use them around the central fire.

Sometimes I thought you were asking me a question. You came close to say that you had gruel for me to eat, mashed pine nuts, the broth of deer meat.

Then I realize that I cannot move my lips. I cannot feel the muscles in my throat or hear the sound of air from my lungs.

I know I am no longer in my tent.

Now I wonder if you are the mammoth necklace, my old friend.

But this does not seem likely. The necklace has already heard these stories, and she would have interrupted me long ago. In truth, the matriarch is not much interested in the lives of human beings.

I think I am already in the earth. I have been covered with red ochre and buried with my awl and ivory needles. Perhaps you are a small beetle drawn to my body, taking it away bit by bit, moving with me deeper into soil.

I do not know if I want to be carried off in so many directions. I have felt my skin stretch thin as I hunted and entered the land, flying over hills, a shimmering net of light and color. Here my skin is stretched so thin that it crumbles and breaks and I crawl away with myself.

My flesh is frightened but my bones are not.

I think the necklace of the matriarch is on my breast. I think Chi won his argument with Crane. I listen for Half Ear's voice. Perhaps she is asleep.

Bloated with gas, suddenly my stomach splits open, and my inside spirit, the essence of willow, slips from my blackened body, rises through soil, and drifts toward the river. I settle in a wet thread of sap. In the spring I will wake to ecstasy.

Now I know who you are. I understand how you can hear words I can no longer speak. In my grave, you cover my mouth. This is a gift from my daughter Ali, from one of her children who wove me a loose basket of willow leaves. Chi put you over my lips. In this way I easily fill you with my story. When I am done and you hold my life in the shape of a bowl, you will tell me your story, everything you learned when you touched the face of Old Man.

Soon Half Ear will wake and we will hear her too, the sound of mammoths running across the plain.

We will listen to the bone awl, the ivory needle, the beetle and the worm.

192 Someday, after a very long time, we will return to the stars. I will greet the bearskin and we will dance, bear and human, by the long white river.

Acknowledgments

In my research, I am grateful for the work of Paul S. Martin and Donald Grayson. I must also thank C. Vance Haynes for his theory that an extended drought in the Southwest just before 10,900 B.P. caused game to congregate at watering holes, where they were more easily killed. Reasonably, the extinction of mammoths in these areas was a two-punch blow, a result of climate change and the human hunter.

Across America, we can still find fluted points from Paleolithic tribes. In *Mammoths, Mastodons, and Elephants*, Gary Haynes suggests that the Clovis population exploded when hunters took advantage of massive mammoth die-offs. His work also gave me information on mammoth biology. George C. Frison has written with authority on Clovis weapons and hunting techniques. I took from Cynthia Moss's book *Elephant Memories* many of my details on mammoth behavior; my fictional character Red Fur is a composite of her research subjects. For other animals, I consulted *Pleistocene Mammals of North America*, by Bjorn Kurten and Elaine Anderson.

For the vegetation of southern New Mexico and eastern

Arizona, I relied mainly on *Packrat Middens,* edited by Julio L. Betancourt, Thomas R. Van Devender, and Paul S. Martin. Their maps show piñon/juniper/oak woodlands where we see grasslands. Montane conifer forests, subalpine forests, and boreal forests followed the higher elevations. Arbitrarily I have assumed a lower woodlands with large expanses of open plain punctuated by trees, suitable to and created by grazing animals.

A note on age: Florida skeletons from 6,000 to 7,000 years ago show that people were living into their sixties at that time. Similarly (over Paul Martin's objection) the few characters in my book who avoid gross injury have been permitted a long life. My narrator Willow mated with her first husband at the age of thirteen and had her first child two years later. If they live, women in her tribe can be grandmothers at thirty and great-grandmothers at forty-five. At the advanced age of sixty, they would commonly suffer from arthritis, cataracts, and bad teeth.

I don't know who wrote "art is theft." A victim of my thievery is Elizabeth Marshall Thomas, the author of two novels, *Reindeer Moon* and *Animal Wife,* as well as four nonfiction books, *The Harmless People, The Warrior Herdsmen, The Hidden Life of Dogs,* and *The Tribe of Cats.* My vision of Paleolithic life and our relationship with animals builds on her work.

Many other writers, most of them Native American, helped shape my thoughts on how people fit into the landscape and how we can claim the land as our home. In writing this book, I was able to live out some of these ideas. It was a lot of fun.